X

W9-CNC-076

THE BIG EAR

ALSO BY ROBIN HEMLEY:

Turning Life into Fiction (practical criticism, Story Press, 1994)

The Last Studebaker (novel, Graywolf Press, 1992)

All You Can Eat (stories, Atlantic Monthly Press, 1988)

The Mouse Town (stories, Word Beat Press, 1987)

THE BIG EAR

Stories by
ROBIN HEMLEY

John F. Blair, Publisher
Winston-Salem, North Carolina

DESIGNED BY LIZA LANGRALL
COVER BY ROYCE BECKER

The paper in this book meets the guidelines
for permanence and durability of the
Committee on Production Guidelines
for Book Longevity of the Council
on Library Resources.

Library of Congress Cataloging-in-Publication Data
Hemley, Robin, 1958–
    The big ear : stories / by Robin Hemley.
        p.   cm.
    ISBN 0-89587-128-9
    1. United States—Social life and customs—20th century—Fic-
tion.
    2. Humorous stories, American.   I. Title.
    PS3558.E47915B5 1995   95-5461
    813'.54—dc20   CIP

*For **Elaine Gottlieb Hemley**
and in memory of
Cecil Hemley*

CONTENTS

ACKNOWLEDGMENTS

I AM GRATEFUL to the following publications in which these stories first appeared. "Wernher von Braun's Last Picnic" appeared in *ACM* (Another Chicago Magazine). "Saint of The Roof Rats" appeared in *Beloit Fiction Journal*. "Independence Boulevard" appeared in *Boulevard*. "Hobnobbing With The Nearly Famous" appeared in *Manoa: A Pacific Journal of International Writing*. "Shinsaibashi" appeared in *Mississippi Valley Review*. "Serenade" appeared in *North American Review*. "The Liberation of Rome" appeared in *North Carolina Humanities*. "Sleeping Over" appeared in *The North Carolina Literary Review*. "The Last Customer" was published by the *North Carolina Writers Network Syndicated Fiction Project*. "The Perfect Word" appeared in *The North Dakota Quarterly*. "My Father's Bawdy Song" appeared in *Ploughshares*. "The Holocaust Party" appeared in *Prairie Schooner* and won the Hugh J. Luke Award. "Letters to the Editor" won a Syndicated Fiction Project Award and was featured on National Public Radio's "The Sound of Writing." "The Big Ear" appeared in *Willow Springs* and won The George Garrett Award for Fiction. It was also reprinted in *The Pushcart Prize XIX*. "A Printer's Tale" appeared in *Story* and won Story's Humor Competition. "An Intruder" appeared in *Witness* and was reprinted in *Best American Humor of 1994*.

My heartfelt thanks go to Beverly Hemley, Mark West, Stephen Kirk, Carolyn Sakowski, Lizzie Grossman, and Anne Czarniecki for their support.

THE BIG EAR

THE BIG EAR, NEARLY AS LARGE AS PETER, and brightly colored, stands out wherever he takes it, but no one really knows what it is, unless they ask. Peter practices withering looks on the people who ask, especially if they're kids. With the seriousness of purpose and steadiness of a Civil War photographer, he stands beside his Big Ear on its black tripod. He pretends to make fine calibrations on the plastic orange cone, bending into it and tapping it with a finger. Most people never get close enough to bother him with questions. That is one of the wonderful things about the Big Ear: it is a powerful device. You can set it up almost as far away from people as you like, two hundred yards, and it still picks up what they're doing. It can listen through windows. It can penetrate plaster walls.

A golf course surrounds the lake; the groundskeepers supposedly use mercury to treat the greens. The mercury leaks down the
hill to the lake, where the fish ingest it, so you're not supposed to
eat fish anymore from here. Before he found out about the mercury poisoning, fishing was Peter's favorite activity. A few weeks
before, he caught fifteen catfish off the dock, and gave them to
a girl he met. He hasn't seen her since, but that, probably, is
just coincidence.

A couple lies by an inlet on the water's edge. They're positioned behind a nearly rotten log. Peter stands on a hill overlook-
ing them. He feels like a general observing a sleeping enemy camp.
He swivels the cone toward the couple. From this distance, he can't
make out their features. In fact, he has not seen the woman at all. The
man's face bobs above the log, and sometimes he reaches out and
grabs at a slender branch rising from the top of the log. Dry rattle,
then a crumbling sound as he strips the branch of its dead leaves.

"You've got to call Catherine," the man says.

A duck calls, the water laps steadily, there is a smacking noise
like chewing gum. From somewhere, Peter picks up the sounds of
Magic 98. "Back-to-back good-time oldies," a cheerful man says,
then drowns. Something metal-sounding snaps.

"Her dog's dying," says a woman's voice.

The couple bursts out laughing. There's a scrabbling sound,
twigs breaking, bodies repositioning themselves. "Oh God," says
the woman, breathless. "That's not what I meant."

"What did you mean?" says the man.

A match flares up and then a long in-suck of breath.

"Now come here. I didn't mean that."

"No, wait. Later."

"What later?"

"Are you going to salad control tonight?" That's what it sounds
like. Salad control. Sometimes, Peter can't make out words too

clearly. Maybe the man meant salad control. Maybe he didn't. If there's one thing Peter's learned since his mother bought him the Big Ear for his birthday, it's that people speak in code. You could have all the Big Ears in the world lined up, and still you wouldn't be able to make sense of what people tell each other. He figures there's something people aren't telling *him*, the clue to the code. Not his teachers, not his mother, not his friends. Whatever it is, he needs to find out soon, before he's too old. It just seems so strange to him, life, the whole nine yards. That's his mom's favorite phrase. She uses it most often on the phone when she talks to Guido. At two in the morning, three, when she thinks Peter's asleep. But he always listens. He thinks she calls Guido so late not only because she wants privacy, but because she wants to wake Guido up. She wants to aggravate him the way he aggravates her. That's love.

She's not hard to hear. Her voice bounces through the whole house. "What do I want, Guido? I'll tell you what. The whole nine yards!"

"Hey, look at that kid up there," the man says, startling Peter.

"What?" The woman sits up, arms folded across her chest. "Where?"

"Up there." The man points at Peter.

Peter pretends he hasn't heard them. If the man starts toward him, he can run off with his Big Ear before the man's halfway up the hill. Peter goes to the front of the cone, leans inside, and makes a fine calibration. Then he swivels the cone straight up toward the sun as though this was his intended target all along. An experiment: sunspots and their means of communication. When he looks next, the couple is gone, or maybe hiding behind the fallen log.

"Did you catch anything?" his mother asks, coming around to the trunk of her Taurus so Peter can stash his gear. Obviously, he's not carrying a fishing pole. Clearly, he's not carrying fish. But his mother seems to see conversation as useful even when it makes no sense. The obvious can never be overstated. Fishing poles, Big Ears, they're all the same to her. What matters is that she's talking. He heard the word for it last year in sixth grade when he was studying government. *Filibuster*. His mother filibusters life. She filibusters words the way Peter's father used to filibuster beer—to fill up the silence in the pit of his stomach.

"No, I didn't catch anything, Mom."

"Oh well. Maybe next time. We've got to hustle. My class is coming over in two hours, and I haven't even bought the booze. How do I look?"

Over the last couple of months, she's been dressing more and more strangely, and it's a little embarrassing bringing friends over. Today, she's wearing too-tight black jeans and a white T-shirt that reads BUTTON YOUR FLY in bold black letters. Over that, she's got a thousand tons of Mexican silver bangles.

"Shouldn't you wear something a little more conservative to teach in?" Peter says.

His mother smiles as though Peter's given her a compliment and says, "They hate me here anyway. So just answer the question. Do I look all right? By the way, I've got to go to Atlanta next week."

Peter doesn't say anything, but gets into the car beside her. She gives him a fleeting look of guilt, tears at a fingernail. "Oh damn," she says when she sees it's bleeding. "I've got to," she says. "This is the last time, I promise. We're going to try to figure out a way to patch things up. If not, that's it. Finis. *A bientôt*."

His mom is always trying to patch things up with her boyfriend—if you want to call him that—Guido. Eunuch, is how she refers to him when things aren't working between them—which is always.

"You're going to need a pretty big patch, Mom," Peter tells her.

She laughs and shakes her head. "Don't I know it, kiddo."

"Who's the lucky gal this time, Mom?" Every time she goes, she leaves him with a different student.

"Oh, you mean the babysitter?" Peter cringes at the word. "You'll meet her tonight. Just your type."

That evening, twelve women sit in the living room, nodding like dashboard figurines to the choppy rhythms of one another's poetry. Peter's mom likes him to sit in on her classes so "you won't grow up to be another prick." She doesn't say it, but she could just as well add "like your father." She says her classes are political with a small *p*, never a large *P*. Usually, Peter reads "X-Men" or "Spiderman" during his mom's classes, but she never seems to notice. Just as long as he "absorbs the ambience." She says the word *ambience* with a slight French accent.

Instead of a comic book, Peter flips through his mail-order gag catalogue tonight. This is where he found the Big Ear. While he half-listens to the student poetry, he checks off the items he'd like to own: joy buzzers, itching powder, fake vomit. There's also a large group of things that squirt—Peter already owns a squirting toilet seat, but would like to add to his repertoire. Of course, the famous squirting flower is in the catalogue, but who wants something as obvious as a fake flower? There are plenty of other squirting things: a transistor radio, a diamond ring, a chocolate bar. The pictures of the squirting products all show someone innocently bending down to take a peek at a friend's diamond ring, or about to bite a generously offered chocolate bar, or to listen to the latest song on a top-forty station. The results are similar. A jet of water from the diamond ring blows out the offending eye. A flood shoots through the ears of the rock fan. A geyser chokes the chocolate lover. And in each picture, at a safe distance from the mayhem, stands a little cartoon guy with a big head and electrocuted hair, grasping himself around the waist, bent over with his knees locked together. "HA HA HA!" is written in bold black letters all around the ad, and in smaller letters are the words, "Thousands of gags for incredibly low prices!" To own all those gags—that would be the whole nine yards.

Tonight, one woman reads a poem about shopping for boyfriends at the Winn-Dixie. She describes some of her boyfriends as canned vegetables, condensed Green Giants who give her botulism. Her old boyfriends are stretched out in the frozen-food case, lewd smiles on their faces. The guy she's dating now is in the fresh-meat section, a butt steak. Everyone laughs at this part except for Peter. How did they get in the frozen-food section in the first place? he wants to know. Were they murdered?

The next woman speaks so softly everyone has to bend close to hear her poem. She has a lilt to her voice and a Southern accent.

Strikebreaker

Your body,
tied to routine like a turbine,
your private Industrial Age
a cotton gin rakes seed.
Blind workers strive
for a world the bosses would never
know or approve of, a new light, lighter
than air machine,
engineering nearly bloodless revolutions.
Still, I'm lucky knowing,
at least, the factory in which I work.
I agitate, pass out
leaflets, never knowing the real conditions
or understanding your demands.

Peter listens quietly throughout the poem, and looks around to see the others' reactions. Almost everyone looks bewildered, except for his mother. She has her hands in front of her face as though she's praying. The rest of the class looks down at their laps or up at the ceiling. A woman next to Peter picks the shag carpet. He glares at her until she looks up and stops.

Peter looks at the woman who read the poem. She has her head tilted slightly.

No one speaks for a second when the poem is finished, but then there's a yelp from the bathroom.

Peter looks around to see if anyone else has noticed, but they're still thinking about the poem. The bathroom door opens and the woman who yelped sits down on the living-room floor again. She looks a little pale, but other than that, acts like nothing unusual has happened to her.

As everyone starts talking about the poem, Peter gets up quietly and goes to the bathroom to check on his gag. When he lifts the toilet seat, the little red bulb with an eyedropper attached isn't there anymore. He checks around and finds it at the bottom of the wastebasket. Peter picks up the bulb and dries it off with some toilet paper. He unscrews the eyedropper from the bulb and runs some water. When the water gets cold enough, he places the bulb under the tap. Then he screws the top on again and places it under the toilet seat with the eyedropper pointing up.

Peter has nothing against his mother's students. In fact, he likes most of them. He would like to talk to them but he's shy.

He presses the toilet seat gently and a thin stream of water shoots up. Good. Hair-trigger action. The illustration in the catalogue for this device shows a man with his pants around his knees tumbling through the air on top of a fountain that shoots up from the toilet.

The next poem is about cutting off some guy's dick and wearing it around the poet's neck. The woman reading this poem is the woman who got squirted with Peter's gag toilet seat. The woman whispers the poem and her hands shake as she reads. She glares at

Peter. She fingers her collar as though the dick is dangling there. She looks like a nun working a rosary.

Peter's mother is staring down at the carpet, shaking her head, rolling her eyes. Peter wants to cover his ears because the poem is so stupid. He sits in a corner against the wall, hugging his knees.

The poet mentions God, sort of. The poem ends with her stamping a foot three times like a horse, slowly, and saying the word *Goddess*.

When it's over, half the students clap, and Peter's mother exhales. "Whew," she says after a moment's silence, "I need a cigarette."

At break, they all go out on the porch. This is where his mother has set up a pony keg for her students and a mountain of Dixie Cups. Peter joins his mother out there. He could have a beer if he wanted. His mother doesn't want him to think drinking's a big deal. But he doesn't want to drink tonight. He wants to watch his mother smoke. His mother always steps out on the porch for her smoke. Even though it's her house, she's considerate of other people's feelings about smoking—and so she smokes outside when people visit.

"Consideration," she's told Peter, "means that you want what's best for other people, not only yourself." Peter wonders why then she doesn't quit smoking, knowing that he hates it.

She's talking to the student who read the poem about the strike-breaker, and Peter stands around listening as though he's interested, but he's really waiting for her to light up.

They start talking and giggling about the poem with the dangling dick. Peter's mother is almost breathless with laughter. "Oh no, not circumcision!" she yells in a stage whisper, clutching her side and holding onto her student for balance.

Peter doesn't understand everything they're talking about. He never does when his mother talks in this language. This is the language she uses with her favorite students. It is a language of raised eyebrows and short laughter, of people and places that Peter doesn't know. It is a language she speaks with confidence. It is the language of absorbing the ambience. Then there is the language of Guido, full of sighs and complaints and accusations. Peter understands neither language; they seem spoken by two completely different people. Sometimes, he thinks his mother is two people—and that neither would like the other if they ever met.

"Don't you want a cigarette, Mom?" Peter says, interrupting them. "Break's almost over."

The student and his mother turn to him at the same time. His mother smiles and says, "Is it? Well, we can take a few extra minutes. This is Nan, Peter. She's going to be babysitting for you when I go to Atlanta."

"I wouldn't call him a baby," Nan says.

"He'll always be *my* baby," says his mom, trying to give him a squeeze, but he squirms out of her reach.

"Cool poem," Peter tells Nan, bobbing his head and not looking at her.

"You liked it?"

Peter has exhausted his ability to discuss literature. He *said* it was cool, but she seems to want him to say more.

"I raised him to be sensitive," says his mother, brushing back some hair from his eyes before he can duck.

"Mom, break's almost up," Peter says.

Nan looks at him and then at his mother. "Is he always this conscientious?"

"Always," says his mother, smiling.

Nan shakes her head wistfully. "I wish you were ten years older," she tells Peter. "I can't wait to see what you'll be like when you're thirty. I'll wait for you."

He wonders if she's kidding. She looks serious.

"I'm too fickle," he says. His mother uses that word when she talks about Guido.

Nan and his mother crack up, then Nan says, "Me, too. We were made for each other." But he thinks she's just kidding.

His mother finally takes out her pack of cigarettes. Peter's not sure if the cigarette she's chosen contains the load, but he made sure that one was sticking up farther then the rest when he replaced it in the pack.

"Mind if I mooch one from you?" Nan asks.

"It's not good for you," Peter says.

"What?" his mother says. "It's not good for her, but it's fine for me?"

"You're hopeless," Peter says.

"Thanks," says his mom.

"Me, too," says Nan, reaching for a cigarette. "I'm hopeless and I'm fickle. I sure am learning a lot about myself tonight. I can't wait to house-sit. This should be an enlightening experience. And you're out in the country, too. I love the country." Nan blows out smoke from her nose and then inhales fresh air.

"I wouldn't call it the country," says Peter's mom. "It used to be the country, back when Joel and I first moved here. All that's left from those days is the well out back."

She launches into an extended history of the subdivision, gesturing over the rail into the dark. Peter listens to everything else around him: the trickle and murmur of conversation from the dozen people crowding the porch. The slopping of drinks. The clean sound of the glass door as it slides open. The pumping of the keg, which seems to pump sounds from the night as well: crickets and a breeze and the rush of the highway a mile off.

The pop seems to come from Nan's finger, and all three of them startle. Nan's sleeve is on fire. He just stares at it. This wasn't supposed to happen. Nan stares at her burning sleeve, too, as though it's something she's imagined. One of his mother's other students stumbles over from the keg and douses Nan's sleeve with beer. Then, without a word, she works her way back to the keg and stands in line for more.

"I'm sorry," Peter says, and he is. He meant to blow up his mother, not Nan.

"I'm so embarrassed," his mother says.

"That's all right, really," says Nan, but he can tell she's upset. This has probably ruined his chances with her.

"Why can't I keep violence out of the picture? Where does he get this from? TV? His genes?" She seems not to be talking to Nan, or anyone else in particular. She's gesturing over the railing, as though filibustering the entire subdivision or a multitude, like the pope in St. Peter's Square.

Peter's mother has been gone nearly all week, and she's only called him once, to tell him she arrived safely. She must be having fun, but Peter doesn't care. He's having fun, too. Nan hasn't held a grudge against him like some of the students his mother's left him with before. He stayed away from these students, skulking in the background, blowing up plastic soldiers with Black Cat fire-crackers in the backyard. Nan's different. For one thing, she's funny. She's taught him the word *indubitably*. He has no idea what it means, but he loves the sound of it. "Indubitably," she says in a British accent and he cracks up.

With Nan, he listens to sounds closer to home.

One night, Peter sets up the Big Ear outside her bedroom and listens to her breathe. The phone rings and Peter freezes.

Nan emerges from the bedroom, rubbing her eyes. She jumps when she sees the big orange cone in front of the door. "My God," she says, hand over her heart. "What the hell is that?"

"My Big Ear."

"Your *what*?"

"Sometimes, I can pick up radio stations late at night," Peter says, looking at the floor.

"Kind of like a satellite dish?" she says.

Peter runs for the phone so he won't have to explain any more.

"Peter," his mother says, breathless. "I'm in love. I met someone in the airport. His name is Antoine."

"What about Guido?"

"Look, I'm staying another week. Antoine has got to go back to France, and I just can't bear the thought of being separated from him before then."

What about me? he wants to say, but instead says, "What about Guido?"

"Look, are you getting along with Nan? Do you like each other?"

"A lot. She says she's going to marry me when I'm thirty."

"See, I told you she was your type."

"What about Guido?"

"Why this sudden interest in Guido? I thought you hated Guido. Anyway, Guido's not giving me what I need, you know, the whole nine yards. With Antoine, at least I get nine yards for two weeks."

"I don't get it," he says. It's true, he hates Guido, but his mother can be awfully tricky. He wants to be sure she's finally gotten over him this time.

"You'll get it when you're older. I know it doesn't make sense, honey, but one thing you've got to understand sooner or later is that no one knows anyone else's thoughts. If we knew each other's thoughts, there would be no need for secrets. There'd be nothing to hide, and people always have something to hide. Guido had his thoughts and I had mine, and that's why I've been messed up for so long. That's over. I promise, honey. No more traveling. I have no idea at all what I want now and I don't expect anything from anyone and I've never been happier. It's crazy, but the world's crazy. It's harmless, so don't worry about me."

Peter hasn't thought about worrying until that moment, but he *is* worried about her. When she gets in a mood like this, she can convince herself to do anything. When she returns, he knows, she'll be so down he'll have to scrape her off the floor. She's met Antoine before, though his name was Robert last time and Clark before that. She'll come back to Guido, and she'll laugh and cry at the same time and say, "God, how could I be so stupid? How could I fall for Antoine's tricks?"

Most afternoons, Peter sets up his Big Ear in the front yard of his house. He points the device down the road, though he doesn't always know what he's listening for.

Nan spends half her days out back, practicing her tae kwon do, the house between them.

At night, they sit up in his mother's room, where Nan is sleeping while Peter's mother is away. They sit cross-legged on the bed, and she sings for him, ancient folk songs about lonesome murderers. For someone who's so small, her voice is deep and rich, and suited to songs of backwoods hollows and hangings. He never asked Nan to sing. It just happened the first night after dinner. After that first night, they were friends. She doesn't only sing, but she talks to him, too. She tells him things about her life that no one has ever told him. Not even his mother. She tells him about a trip last year to Europe with a man named Phil, and how they argued, and how he left her in the middle of this bridge with no money and no way to get home.

"What did you do?"

"I managed."

"How could he do that?" Peter asks. He imagines Nan standing in the middle of a giant white bridge with pillars topped by lions' heads, and a bent figure in a trench coat hurrying away.

Peter remembers the day his father left them. They were in the kitchen. Peter's mother said he was threatened by women, and his father laughed.

"You know it goes both ways," he said.

"Yes it does," she answered calmly. "I'm not denying that. It's natural to feel threatened. Why shouldn't we feel threatened? That's the only thing we're experts at, inspiring fear and weathering it."

"I'm not afraid of you," he'd said.

"You're not listening," she said calmly, her arms folded, but Peter could see she was trembling.

Peter takes out a pack of Wrigley's gum from his pocket, but if you look closely at the wrapping, you notice that it doesn't really say Wrigley's but Wriggles. So Peter always feels justified when he offers people this gum. If they're paying attention, they'll notice the fake name and won't fall for the trick, a mousetrap that snaps on your finger when you pull the stick of gum from the pack.

He thinks of the last person he offered the gum to, a girl named Susan MacNamara. Susan wanted to go steady with him a few months back, and he agreed, but he didn't know what he was getting into. One day, she led him down to a gully near her house, to a hollowed-out log where she said she used to sit and think. She told him she had a surprise for him and then kissed him.

"Ow," Peter said.

Susan pulled back. "Ow? Why'd you say 'ow'?"

"I don't know," he said, feeling ashamed. "I thought you were going to do something to me."

"Peter Costello. You're not supposed to say 'ow' when a woman kisses you."

"Okay," he said, and closed his eyes and puckered his lips. But she didn't feel like kissing him now. That's when he offered her the gum.

"Phil sounds mean," Peter tells Nan.

Nan looks up at the ceiling and says, "I never thought of Phil as mean when I was with him. He didn't do anything outwardly cruel. But it was inside of him all the time. To this day, he probably gets a kick out of the thought of abandoning me like that, thinks it made him a man. If I ever see him again . . . All my life I've been involved with murderers. Part of the attraction of the relationship was the pain, but I really think that's the last time I'm going to let that happen. That's why I'm taking tae kwon do, not so much for the self-defense, but for the confidence. I *was* taking judo. Judo teaches you to use the attacker's own force against him, but you know what? It doesn't work. We've been going that route much too long. I'm never going to put myself in that position again. You know that Billie Holiday song, 'God Bless the Child That's Got Its Own'?"

Peter shakes his head, entranced.

"Do you want to hear it?" She starts to sing, but stops and looks at him seriously. "You're not going to be that way, are you? You wouldn't leave anyone stranded in the middle of a bridge."

"Not you," Peter answers.

She narrows her eyes and says, "Not anyone."

"Okay," Peter says.

"Promise?"

Peter nods.

Nan bends over and kisses Peter's forehead, strands of her hair tickling his face. He doesn't understand how someone could hate her as much as Phil must have. He imagines himself and Nan together when he's thirty, watching TV, picking up conversations on the Big Ear.

"I like this," Nan says.

"Me, too."

"Men should stay twelve, don't you think?"

"Indubitably," Peter says.

"Come to think of it," she says, but doesn't finish the thought. "Oh, you have gum?" she says, reaching for it.

"It's my last piece," he says. "I'm saving it." Peter puts the gum back in his pocket. He knows how selfish that sounds. He'd like Nan to read his mind, to know she doesn't really want this fake gum. She smiles and touches his leg and says, miraculously, "That's fine. I don't need it."

Peter hears the telephone ringing. It's his mother. He knows her ring, and he knows what she's going to say before she says it, that things with Antoine didn't work out, that she misses Guido, that she's returning home early. Peter looks at Nan and she looks at him, and for some reason, they both burst out laughing. He wishes that it could always be like this, that he could relay and receive telepathic messages, speak different languages, that distance didn't matter, that every nerve in his body was attuned to the slightest sounds.

LETTERS TO
THE EDITOR

THE MAN SOUNDED POLITE, like he was calling to help out Gloria. "We know where you live, bitch." She almost expected him to add, "So don't go to any trouble giving us directions, ya hear?"

She hung up on him.

She found her mother on the sun porch, reading the newspaper.

"Guess what, Gloria?" her mother said.

"The baby Jesus appeared before you and told you about the sale at Belk's?"

Gloria's mother put down the paper and said, "Very funny, missy, but someday God's going to read that back to you from his scrapbook." She took a sip of orange juice. "What sale?" she asked.

Gloria's mom had kept a scrapbook when Gloria was little, but

God had taken over the cutting and pasting duties when Gloria was fifteen and her mother had become a partner at Heritage USA. Gloria's mother had an uncanny knack for foretelling a church's downfall by joining it. After Heritage collapsed, she'd cast her lot with the Reverend Jimmy Swaggart. Now she was between churches. She was trying to decide between Oral Roberts and Robert Schuller. Both had built immense churches, and she believed that anyone who could build something "as mighty and huge as the Crystal Cathedral or Oral Roberts University must be close to God."

"Yeah, like the Tower of Babel," Gloria had said, but her mother simply blinked at her.

"There's no sale, Mother. In my country, is called joke, sarcasm." Gloria went around the table and kissed her mother's cheek.

"They printed my letter."

Gloria snatched the newspaper from her mother. It was already turned to the editorial page, and there it was in the middle under the headline "Curb Homosexual Menace."

> Many of our nation's problems could be solved if we would only look to the source, the homosexuals taking over our schools, entertainment industry, and even our government! Homosexuals spread crime, drugs, diseases, and bad feelings. Even some churches are ordaining homosexuals to preach in the pulpit! If we do not do something soon, we will be taken over by this menace, which is worse than Communism and Secular Humanism combined. Now that we have defeated the Russians, let's defeat the enemy at home!
>
> *Vonnie Truitt*
> *Charlotte*

Gloria put the paper down. She knew the letter by heart. Her mother had come bounding into her room a few days ago and cheerily said, "Oh, Gloria! There's something I'd like you to print out for me." That had been her first mistake, agreeing to print it. Then her mother had asked her to set the letter out front for the mailman to pick up. Gloria thought of not mailing it, but telling her she had. But no matter how onerous her mother's opinions, she couldn't stop her from expressing them. So she placed the letter by the mailbox. An hour later, she changed her mind, decided there were some opinions that didn't need to be voiced. But the letter was already gone by the time she reached the mailbox. It's such a crank letter, she thought. They won't print it.

Now she felt stupid. Of course, they love crank letters. And here was her mother's name as plain as day on the editorial page of the *Charlotte Observer*, and everyone at school, all her professors and friends, would look at her and wonder if she felt the same.

"You know what just happened?" she said to her mother. "Someone called up and said, 'We know where you live.'" She left off the word *bitch* because that's all her mother would have heard.

"Don't worry. Nothing will happen," Vonnie Truitt said. "Everyone knows homosexuals are cowards and sissies."

Her mother had not always been like this. There'd been a time before Heritage, in those blissful years when Gloria's father was still alive, that Gloria's mother had made sense. In those days, she'd believed in busing and a woman's right to an abortion, and her favorite program on TV was *M*A*S*H*. She'd even believed in gay rights. Gloria's father had been the conservative one. Back then, Gloria had been able to hate her father in a pleasant, reassuring way, a hate that made her feel good about herself and her place in the world. Whatever his views, she knew hers were just the opposite. She and her mother had had an alliance against him, broken by his death, when Gloria's mother switched and started taking on his views like an inheritance, a trust fund. Gloria went through some changes, too. She believed, for instance, she had killed him. The night he had his heart attack, he and Gloria had been arguing. This was a week after Mao died, and Gloria was saying that capitalism and democracy were not always best for developing nations, that at least Mao was feeding a billion people (no mean feat) and had vastly improved the lot of women in his country. This was during Gloria's first stint as a student, when she was college age. Gloria had been taking a class on China, and was simply stating to her father the sensible views of her professor. Her father had questioned why she was wearing a black armband, and so she was explaining things to him.

Gloria's mother never called it a heart attack. She said that his heart had "suffered an insult." That was her mother's way of speaking, but Gloria wondered if that was her way of blaming Gloria, too. In all those years, Gloria had never asked her mother directly.

Gloria brought the paper with her to school, and when she ran into friends and professors and they said, "How's it going?" she waved the paper in front of their noses and said, "This is how it's going. My mother wrote this letter." They expressed sympathy, horror. "You know what my wake-up call was this morning? 'We know where you live, bitch.' I wanted to say, 'No, you have the wrong bitch. The bitch you want is my mother.'" One of her profs handed back the paper and said, "That's so scary," but she wasn't sure whether he was talking about the threat or her mother's letter.

After school, Gloria went to the bank to cash a rent check from one of her mother's tenants. She didn't know any of the tellers at this branch. The teller who waved her over to his window was a slim man with a mustache. The man was tall and stood ramrod straight. He looked like a rookie: alert, smiling, but slightly officious. She hated bank tellers, not individually, but as a class. Maybe they should be lined up and shot, like Mao did with landlords after he came to power. Ah, Mao.

The teller must have been reading her thoughts. He studied

her signature, then asked if her address was correct. He took the check and brought it to another teller, and the two of them whispered about her.

Finally, he came back with the manager and stared sternly at her while the manager, a heavyset man with a toupee, asked her to sign her name and show them some more ID.

"What's the problem?" she asked.

"It's for your own protection, ma'am," the manager said.

"Oh, all right." She showed them her license and signed a piece of paper. The manager nodded at the rookie and the teller stepped back to the window, folded his hands, and said, "I'm sorry, but we'll have to hold your check until it clears."

"For how long?" she said. "My mother and I need that money. I've never had any problems before."

He smiled at her. "Ten days. I apologize for the inconvenience, but this is done for our customers' protection."

"Ten days. Give me back the check. I'll go to my regular branch."

"It's already in the system. If you'd like to speak with one of our personal bankers . . ."

"Give me back my check," she said. "We need it." But it was no use. The bastard just kept saying it was already in the system. It sounded like he was talking about some bug, a cold that had to work its way through the system before the system got better.

"Have people been calling and threatening you all day?" Gloria asked her mother when she returned home.

"Why should they do that?" her mother asked. She was sitting at the dining-room table, biting reflectively on the end of a pen.

"I don't know," said Gloria. "I just thought a declaration of war against an entire demographic group might elicit a little response."

Gloria's mother looked up in the air and said, "A few people have called. One man used some very harsh language. I told him that Pope Pius VI used to burn homosexuals at the stake, and I say good riddance."

"How terrifying," Gloria said.

"Of course, the pope isn't much better," her mother said. "And how was your day?"

"Fine, except for the fact that the stupid bank wouldn't cash our check. They want to hold it for ten days. I don't know how we'll get by."

"That's only a quarter as long as it rained in the time of the Flood," her mother replied.

Gloria sat down at the table with her mother. They had talked before, countless times, but today Gloria was determined to understand her mother. The letter and phone call had thrown her off-balance. Most of the time, she simply accepted her mother as she was. They ignored their differences much better than she and her father had. "Why have you changed? You used to be different before Dad died."

"I *was* different."

"But what made you change? And I'm not talking about seeing the light. What exactly made you change?"

"I saw the light."

"Did it have something to do with me? And don't say it didn't."

"It didn't."

"But do you have to hate other people who think differently? And don't tell me you hate the sin but love the sinner. I know that somewhere inside you is a tolerant, good person. I wouldn't live with you if I didn't think that. Why did you write that letter?"

"I hate the sin but love the sinner."

"How am I going to get through to you?"

Vonnie Truitt placed both hands on the table and pushed herself out of her seat. She smiled down at Gloria and said, "Oh my, it's almost suppertime and I haven't even started anything. I've been working all afternoon on this letter." She pointed to the piece of paper on the table.

"What now?" Gloria said, reaching for the letter.

> Dear Editor,
> If we could stop Yankees from coming down here and stealing our jobs and corrupting our children with their Humanistic philosophies, the South would be in much better shape than it is. Yankees should stay in their own backyards instead of telling us how things ought to be done. We don't need Yankees telling us whether or not we can fly the Confederate flag at the state capitol. It would surprise me a lot if a paper like yours, which is run by a staff of atheists and Yankees, decided to print this letter.
>
> *Vonnie Truitt*
> *Charlotte*

"What do you want to do now? Start the Civil War again?"

"You mean the War of Northern Aggression," her mother said, walking into the kitchen.

Gloria followed. "You're doing this to get back at me," she said, waving the letter at her mother.

"Don't be silly," her mother said.

Gloria was trembling. She held the letter above her head like a battle flag. "You still blame me, don't you?"

"For Pete's sake, Gloria. You're not making any sense these days. I don't know about this university. I knew they'd put ideas in your head."

"No one puts ideas in my head," Gloria said. "I have my own ideas."

"I have ideas, too."

"But they're not your ideas," Gloria said. "They're not. You didn't used to be this way."

"Who pays for your college?" Gloria's mother asked.

"Don't try to get around this, Mother."

"Who pays for your living expenses? If it wasn't for me . . ."

"Admit it, Mother. You blame me."

"Let's not talk about this," her mother said, turning around and walking to the refrigerator. "We get along fine, don't we? Why are you trying to upset me?" She opened the vegetable drawer and took out a head of cauliflower wrapped in plastic.

"Admit it," Gloria said, and started to tear her mother's letter.

Her mother slammed the refrigerator door and marched over to Gloria. She tried to snatch the letter away, but Gloria held it over her head.

"Admit it," Gloria said, smiling. She felt calm and completely justified.

Her mother's face was red and she screamed, "Admit what? What are you trying to do? Drive me to an early grave, too?"

Gloria dropped the letter and it floated down like a leaf and settled underneath the kitchen table. Gloria's mother got down on all fours and reached for the letter. She wouldn't look at Gloria, but Gloria could see her face. She hadn't *really* expected her mother to admit it, but there it was.

"Mother," Gloria said weakly. She couldn't believe it. How could her mother blame her? Didn't some things in life simply happen, outside of human cause and effect? And what if she *was* to blame? How could she live with herself?

The doorbell rang. Her mother stood up and placed the letter on the table. "Mother," Gloria said. "Look at me."

Her mother wouldn't look. "Go see who's at the door," she said.

Gloria's mother tore the plastic from the cauliflower and started snapping off the florets.

The doorbell rang again. When she opened the door, she saw a man in a suit. The porch light hadn't been turned on yet, so his face was slightly hidden in shadow.

Before she could speak, a wave of pink paint sloshed over her head. The paint covered her face, dripped down her back, and streamed down her front. The man gave a war whoop and dropped the bucket on the porch. The bucket clattered off the stoop and into the azalea bushes. The man ran across the lawn and into his car. He was gone in a second.

"Who is it?" Gloria's mother yelled from the kitchen.

Gloria stood with the door open, pink paint dripping onto her mother's carpet. She wasn't sure what had just happened. She was thinking about her father. She was thinking that nothing is simple, that you don't get to choose who you are. She'd always thought it was her choice, but now she knew it wasn't.

"Who is it?" her mother said again.

"I don't know," Gloria said, closing the door. "A man. It could have been anyone."

"What did he want?" her mother said.

"I don't know," Gloria said, paint gumming up her eyes and the corners of her mouth. "You'll have to ask him."

She tracked pink paint across her mother's carpet. The trail would remain. The footprints led to her door, where anyone who wanted could find her.

MY FATHER'S BAWDY SONG

RIGHT AWAY, I STARTED MEETING PEOPLE who knew my brother. A bank teller cashing a traveler's check for me was one. She gave me a half-glance when I passed the check through the window. Then she noticed my last name and slowly lifted her eyes, as though I was someone she should know. "You related to Owen?" she asked.

"My half-brother," I said. I could have simply said my brother, but I never did. I only thought of him as half a brother, whose features I had forgotten long ago.

"We went to school together," the bank teller continued. "Owen and me. That was ages ago." She shook her head. "I never see him," she said suddenly in an accusing tone. "Tell him I never see him. Tell him he should open an account here."

"Okay, if I see him," I said.

I had told my half-brother I was going to spend my summer weekends in Montauk. My girlfriend, Leslie, and some of her friends were chipping in on the rent of a bungalow for the summer. This was a getaway, a place to relax and swim and walk along the beach. I had sent him a letter, but he hadn't replied, not even a phone call. Maybe I hadn't given him enough time to respond. I wanted to see him, though he didn't seem to want to see me. So I hadn't tried to get in touch with him right away.

"Owen Bonnin," she said slowly in a mildly surprised way.

For a moment, we looked at each other and smiled. I didn't know what to say. My only connection to her was through Owen, whom I hadn't seen in nearly twenty years, not since our father's funeral. I say *our* father, though even now that sounds strange, and I want to say *my* father. But standing there, I felt a little fraudulent, as though the last name on the traveler's check didn't belong to me, at least not in Montauk.

She must have read the doubt on my face because she looked again at the check and then at me. Without any hint of awkwardness, she said, "You know, you don't look like him." After a moment, she added in a more impersonal tone, "May I see some ID?"

A week later, at a party in Bridgehampton, I met a woman who had known my father when he lived in Montauk in the late forties. The woman, whose name was Ione Perry, swooped out of nowhere, interrupting the conversation I was having with my friends, and led me off to the kitchen in a flutter of reminiscences.

"Someone told me you were here," she said as we stood by a table with hors d'oeuvres on it. "When I heard, I just had to meet you." She stood and looked at me from head to toe. "Stanley's son," she said, and started spreading pâté on Wasa bread.

She laughed and kept on talking as I nodded and tried to follow. The woman was needle-thin and wore a dashiki and long gold earrings in the shape of tuning forks. She flourished the Wasa bread in front of her as though it were a riding crop to point and slice for dramatic effect. She seemed to emphasize at least one word in every sentence, and when she did so, her mouth stretched in a grimace that revealed a tiny set of teeth encased in the most voluminous gums I'd ever seen. "I'll *never* forget the sight of Stanley pushing Owen in his stroller along the beach. Owen must have been two, and the poor boy looked so *baffled*, because, you know, it's not *easy* pushing a stroller through the sand. It kept getting *stuck*, and Owen was holding on for *dear* life, but not crying. He *never* cried. He just looked so *baffled*, as though he was saying, 'Well, I certainly hope *he* knows where he's going.' But really, I'm afraid that *neither* did. *Certainly* not Stanley. A *dear*, dear man. And *absolutely* determined to make headway with that stroller."

Ione held her Wasa bread aloft and balanced against me while slightly caressing my shoulder. "Have you tried the goose liver?" she screamed suddenly. "Here, you must."

I put my hand in front of my face and smiled.

"No, really, you must," she said, and I knew I must or she'd never leave me alone. As I took a bite, I wondered what my father must have thought about her. Had she always been this annoying? I wondered what her relationship with my father had been. Acquaintance? Lover? That must have been it. Anyone this persistent couldn't have been anything else.

"Stanley taught me my first bawdy song," Ione told me. "Would you like to hear it?"

I wanted to hear it. I was hungry for any information about my father she might have. Whenever I met someone who had known my father, I could listen to them for hours. Whenever I heard some new story about him, I felt like some explorer, like Marco Polo, traveling past the farthest reaches of ancient and distant empires, hearing rumors of coronations and calamity, wondering what these rumors had to do with me.

> Her name was Lil, and she was a beauty
> She lived in a house of ill repu-ty
> Gentlemen came from far to see
> Lillian in her dishabille
> Lillian in her dishabille
>
> With branches in Brazil and Haiti
> She decided to incorpora-ti
> She was the president and she
> Was also the secre-tary
> Was also the secre-tary
>
> Then one day our Lil grew skinny
> The trouble it was endocrin-e
> Her glands they failed when work was done
> From over stimula-shi-on
> From over stimula-shi-on

As people passed through the kitchen for drinks and hors d'oeuvres, Ione sang my father's bawdy song. People smiled and even clapped, but no one stopped for more than a minute. It was clear to everyone this song was meant to be sung to me alone.

The next day, I called my half-brother. "Sure, let's meet up," he said without surprise or apology for not answering my letter. "I'll swing by in half an hour."

After fifteen minutes had passed, I went outside and waited. Leslie didn't like that. As I walked out the door, she said, "Are you embarrassed for him to meet me?"

"Of course not."

"I assume he can walk and talk and get out of his car and knock on the door."

"For God's sake, he's my half-brother," I said.

"Oh no, not that," she said with a horrified look, and put the back of her hand to her forehead. "Not the dreaded half-brother."

"That's not what I meant," I said, "and you know it." I couldn't believe she had such a hard time understanding why I'd like to meet him alone. It had nothing to do with her. I just hadn't seen him in so long. As I stood there, her lack of understanding snowballed in my mind, and I started thinking all kinds of crazy thoughts. I started thinking that this was just like Leslie, that this was emblematic of all our problems. If I chewed my Cheerios on the right side of my mouth instead of my left, she'd be sure to catch the switch, sure she'd said something to make me do it. We hadn't been together long, and neither of us was sure what the other had in mind.

I went outside alone. I waited and fumed, but then the fuming died off and I just waited.

Fifteen minutes, twenty-five, forty minutes passed, and still no one who could pass for a relation of mine drove by. I wondered if something had happened to him. Maybe I'd somehow forgotten to give him the address, but no, I distinctly remembered giving it to him. Three times in the course of our conversation. Maybe I'd said something that upset him. But what could that have been? He might have been upset that I hadn't ever come to Montauk before to visit him. But then he'd never visited me in the city. Maybe he had no intention of getting together with me at all, and had just thought it would serve me right to make me wait. Maybe it would. I started trying to explain myself to Owen in my mind. It has nothing to do with you, I told him. It's just that we've led such different lives for so long. If something could have come of our relationship, wouldn't it have happened before now?

Still, I wanted him to show up. If he didn't, the fraction of our brotherhood would be halved again. I was ready to wait for the rest of my life. No one ever had me in such a powerful grip as Owen had me in then.

As I waited, I thought about my father's life. There was so much of it I knew nothing about, especially from the period in which Owen fit. All I knew about Owen's mother, for instance, was what my mother told me. Whatever my mother said about her was always prefaced with, "Oh, she's an awful woman." Despite that, my mother rarely volunteered much more information. She acted as though it hadn't been a marriage at all, but a night in the drunk tank, a boy's first shave with cause and effect. A bad night, no doubt about it, but it could have been worse.

Beyond that, I was able to piece together few facts.

After an hour, a lime green taxi station wagon pulled up in front of me. With its tail fins and round brake lights, it looked like it was from the early sixties. Written on the door in white paint was the name of a local hotel, The Montalker, and its telephone number. I realized I must have looked like I needed a taxi, just standing in front of a house. Maybe someone nearby had called one to take them to the train station.

I bent down and looked into the front seat. "I don't need a taxi," I said.

"Yes you do," the driver said. "Get in."

I stared at him without saying a word. He didn't look exactly like my father, but enough to frighten me a little. For a moment, I had the impression that this cabdriver *was* my father, and that the two of us were now going to go on some strange metaphysical drive along the beach during which the fare box would click away at a mad rate. Guiltily, I'd know I could never afford it.

"Owen?" I said with a little too much disappointment showing.

If he hadn't been my brother, I wouldn't have wanted to share a cab with him. He looked like an aged lifeguard gone to beer nuts, steroids, and LSD. His eyes were large and glassy. He had a bushy black mustache and eyebrows and hair growing out of his ears, but the top of his head was a half-moon of baldness, which he partially covered with a blue beret. He wore flip-flops, baggy white shorts, and a faded yellow polo shirt with a loose mass of threads hanging over his heart where the insignia should have been.

"I hear you're an architect, too," Owen said as soon as I'd taken a seat beside him.

"Excuse me?" I said, hardly hearing him. It was the face that got me, the roundness of it, that perfect circle I remembered dimly. The scratchiness of his stubble, the warm breath that spoke soft riddles and sang songs off-key. The eyes also. Blue. Even the same crow's-feet. I was astounded at how much came back to me.

"You're an architect also," he repeated.

The word *also* worried me, spoken like an accusation.

"Not an architect in the sense you mean," I said, a little flustered.

He laughed. "Oh, an architect in the best sense of the word."

"I'm employed by the state," I said. "I work on low-income hous-ing. It's a misconception that architects are rolling in the money."

Owen nodded through this little speech of mine. He looked at me steadily, his eyes hard, jaw firm, and I realized how patronizing I must sound to him. After all, he knew what an architect was. He had lived with Dad longer than me.

I had a strange thought. I wondered if Leslie was watching me from the window, and if so, what she thought I was doing. In a cab driven by a half-brother I didn't know. For all she knew, I might have called a cab to take me to the station.

"Where do you want to go?" he asked me like a cabdriver.

"I hadn't thought about it," I told him. "It's your town."

He smiled. "So you want me to show you the sights?"

"Sure."

"Or we could just sit here," he said.

"We could."

"Making small talk. You could ask me what *I* do for a living," he said, and laughed.

I didn't know what my brother had against me, but he apparently didn't like me. We'd established that much. But I was curious about him, and I wouldn't have extricated myself from the situation even if I could have. He started the car and we headed off toward town, a couple of miles downhill, past Montauk Manor, a sprawling hotel that had been a calamity of the Depression, and had never been successfully developed.

He pulled up in front of a tiny bungalow near the center of Montauk. "Dad and Mom's first house," he said. "All the tourists want to see it. They couldn't care less about Dick Cavett's place or Edward Albee's."

Owen took off his beret. Inside was a photograph and he handed it to me. It showed my father, skinny and in his early twenties, sitting on a boulder among the breakers, and smiling broadly.

"Here," he said.

"I can have it?" I asked.

"No," he said like I was crazy. "It's mine."

Owen popped the photograph of Dad back into his beret.

We drove toward the dunes and parked. We sat like shy lovers, saying very little, watching the gulls hover over the sand. I had no sense of ever being here before, but knowing that my father had lived here, I felt it was in some way my natural home.

"Dad was stationed on Long Island during the war," Owen said, beginning his story. He must have intuitively known that's what I wanted, his story, the places I'd been left out of. "Somewhere near the Shinnecock Indian Reservation."

"I never understood that," I said. "I mean, he was trained as an architect."

Owen laughed. "All he did during the entire war was test ordnance, blowing up fake bridges that spanned the sand, detonating clam beds offshore, and stomping on concrete bunkers with gigantic charges of dynamite. An obscure but necessary task for the war effort. I don't know exactly how he met my mom, but I can just imagine her watching his solitary bombing from some sand dune at a safe distance. A courtship dance consisting of the male blowing things up to attract the female's attention, the sand erupting, sending out an invitational spray to all the girls in the area.

"After the war was over, they married and moved here, where my grandfather owned a hotel. They were happy for a while."

That's not what I had heard. My mother told me that soon after they were married their problems started. My father wanted to return to the city to find work as an architect, but his wife wanted him to stay in Montauk and take over her father's hotel.

"Their marriage ended when I was only six," Owen said.

I was only three when he died.

One of the few things my mother told me about the divorce was that in those days you couldn't just get divorced. Someone had to take the blame. In this case, it was my father. "He agreed to everything she wanted," my mother told me. "He agreed to be the villain, and let her say that he'd been having an affair." A cautionary tale.

"He left her high and dry," Owen said. "Lucky she had the hotel to fall back on."

"That doesn't sound like him," I said. I had to defend him. It was obvious that Owen had absorbed his mother's bitterness over our father, that whatever information he'd received was slanted. Even stranger, Owen was looking as though he blamed me, as though I was his father, not his father's other son.

"How would you know?" he said.

I didn't know how to handle such bitterness. I told Owen that maybe I should be heading back, that Leslie was expecting me to cook that night. "Shrimp curry," I said.

"You have to see the hotel. You can call her from there. It's the main attraction on the tour."

It's strange, but I hadn't even thought about going to the hotel. That didn't seem like my father's territory, and I knew Owen's mother was still alive. She wasn't someone I wanted to meet. But on the drive to the hotel, he didn't say anything about her.

The Montalker was up a hill above a fish-processing plant. It needed paint and had an old wooden sign, just the kind of place I would love to have stayed in. Inside, there were movie posters all around. The hotel looked like something from the forties. The windows faced west. A black Naugahyde bar stood in the center, with scratched and scarred wooden tables surrounding it. For a moment, I was sorry that my father had let it go. But what was I thinking?

"You want some chowder?" Owen said. "You should have a bowl. The best thing on the menu."

Owen seemed to be on good terms with the bartender, a woman about ten years younger than he. He leaned over the bar and kissed her. She wore a kind of ruffled Spanish-looking dress with white and red and little embroidered flowers. Her hair was a frizzy cloud around her face.

Owen grabbed a couple of glasses and filled them with beer as he leaned over the bar. The woman regarded him critically.

"Where's Jessica?" he asked.

"Upstairs, asleep, where she should be. Your mother wore her out beachcombing. And the ticks. You know how many ticks I pulled off that child? Seventeen."

"How many were on my mother?" Owen asked. He set down a beer in front of me and clinked my glass with his.

"It's not a contest."

"Okay, I'll talk to her."

"It's just that your mother's getting . . . Well, I'm afraid for *her*."

"I'll talk to her."

The woman shrugged. Then she looked over my way and smiled. "You must be Jack."

"Oh yeah, this is Jack," said Owen.

This was Marie. He hadn't told me anything about her, or his child, and I hadn't asked. Not that he'd asked about my personal life either. He didn't know about Leslie, and I hadn't felt a need to tell him anything. We weren't strangers. We knew each other in a deeper way. The details didn't matter much.

He wasn't married, but I was impressed that Marie was with him and he had a child. I wondered where his mother was. I wondered if she was purposely avoiding me. I didn't know what I'd say when I met her. I never was good at small talk, especially with a woman who probably wished I'd never been born.

"It's June 21st," Owen said to me, sounding in a good mood. He took a sip of his beer. "You know what that is?"

"Something to do with Dad?"

"It's Midsummer Night," he said. Owen set down his beer mug and looked out the window. "Not everything has to do with Dad."

Owen and I sat looking out that window, drinking beer after beer. The jukebox seemed perfect, and made me feel more sentimental than I'd felt all summer. A little sentimentality now and then isn't bad for the circulation. Willie Nelson sang "Georgia on My Mind." And then the Ames Brothers sang "Paper Moon." And Teresa Brewer sang a Tommy Dorsey medley. The sun wouldn't set that night until 8:25, Owen said. It was only 7:20, and I'd already polished off four beers. We had a ways to go, Owen and me. We sat at the two-seater table, saying nothing, and I observed with fondness all the strange couples at the horseshoe bar. There was one young couple, healthy and tan. She ran her fingers through his hair, which was short and sandy, and then she fondled his sunglasses hanging around his neck. And then she pinched the wrinkles in his shirt.

"You don't look like Dad," Owen told me.

"Everyone says I look like my mother."

"You have his voice, his eyes," he said.

"Where's your mother?" I asked.

"I don't know. Upstairs reading probably."

"Doesn't she want to meet me?"

"I don't know," he said. "She doesn't know you're here."

I might have thought he'd purposely avoided telling her, that he thought my presence would cause her too much pain. But I doubt it was that at all. I'm sure he just forgot, that it wasn't important enough. I couldn't believe it, that I was that unimportant to him. But then I thought about it. Had he been important to me? I wanted to be significant to him without the necessity of his being significant to me. I wanted him to feel jealous, but I felt jealous of him, sitting in his hotel, looking at his girlfriend, his sunset, his Midsummer Night, his sentimental moment.

I made some excuse and stumbled out into the dark and down the hill past the fish-processing plant, and back up another hill by Montauk Manor. All the way home, I tried to remember the song that Ione Perry had sung, my father's bawdy song, but all that came back to me were the words "Lillian in her dishabille." What exactly was "dishabille" anyway? "Lillian in her dishabille!" I shouted to the tune of "Minnie the Moocher," as though I knew exactly what it meant, and wanted the world to savor its meaning with me.

Maybe it was the influence of the song, or the beer, or the feelings that had come forth that night, or maybe the worry on Leslie's face when I returned home—but I started thinking about the future and our life together. Leslie went through the litany of things that might have happened to me, that I might have drowned, or been run over, or been torn apart by one of the dogs the neighbors never tied up. What was worse, she thought, I might have left her. "I saw you get into a cab. I didn't know where you went."

"Let's get married," I suggested.

I was always afraid to marry because of my father's failed first marriage, sure I carried in my blood whatever had caused the problems, some genetic flaw. A werewolf's curse. Leslie knew I was drunk and so she didn't take my proposal seriously.

All that summer I saw my brother, usually in his cab picking up tourists at the station. We waved to each other a lot and smiled. "Stop by the hotel sometime," he told me.

I'm *still* afraid of marriage, even though I'm married, though not to Leslie, and have a child. I wonder if my father's blueprint is there, if twenty years after my death, my son will take a cab ride with another half-brother, and he will think he's meeting me again in the other. "What was that question," he will wonder, "that I've been dying to ask you all my life? And why does it seem so unimportant now?"

HOBNOBBING
WITH THE
NEARLY FAMOUS

DANIEL BOONE PRESIDED OVER A FAMOUS NAMES CLUB. Shirley Temple, Paul McCartney, Richard Nixon, Ronald Reagan, and Amelia Earhart belonged to the club as well. Others had less prestigious names, less prestigious because they were more common: four George Washingtons, three Andrew Jacksons, and two John Kennedys. Or less prestigious because their names were not spelled in a famous way: Elvis Paisley, Albert Einsteen, Walt Disnei, Alfred Hitchkoch. After much debate and a threatened schism between the correctly spelled members and the nearly correct, led by the hot-headed and contentious Albert Einsteen, the nearly correct were elevated from observer status and given full recognition. Others were not so blessed. Someone named Norman Ruth tried to gain membership, claiming he was nicknamed "the Babe." Another person swore that everyone called her Madonna. From time to time, people with names that were merely unusual or striking tried to join the club. These people seemed a bit pathetic to Daniel. They had no grounds for applying for membership. A Candy Kane had applied and so had a woman named April Showers. Enough was enough. Already, the bylaws had been compromised by Einsteen and his cohorts, and Daniel, as president, refused to hear their appeals.

Like most members of the club, Daniel looked nothing at all like his namesake, the historical Boone. Nor did he resemble Fess Parker. Daniel was short and burly, with a chubby face and a close-cropped reddish beard. He wore crooked wire-rims that he rarely cleaned, had lost the case for them, in fact. His glasses were always slipping, and he was constantly pushing them back into position. If he looked at all like anyone famous, it was Richard Dreyfuss, but only around the eyes and the mouth.

The members of the club didn't simply go around imitating the famous people whose names they shared, though some of that went on at meetings. Richard Nixon did a great imitation of the president, puffing up his cheeks, making the V sign, hunching his shoulders, and scowling. But that was as far as it went. He looked a bit like Nixon, but when he spoke, the illusion shattered. His voice was not the growling motor of Richard Milhous, but more the manic whine of Richard Simmons.

Much of the time at meetings was spent in serious discussion of the trials and responsibilities of owning a famous name. These discussions were Daniel's favorite part of the weekly meetings. The dialogue had started by accident when the callous Einsteen caused Shirley Temple to burst into tears by singing "On the Good Ship Lollipop" when she was introduced. Shirley had blanched and started sobbing uncontrollably, saying, "No one ever takes me seriously."

This incident had cast a pall over the nearly famous at the meeting, but some good came out of it because the members realized the true reason they were getting together: not solely for the novelty, but also to share their thoughts on the unfairness of being shackled to another person's fame.

The club was Daniel's lifework. He had founded it and nurtured it, and spent most of his days thinking about it. By day, he worked for the Social Security Administration in a nook where he wasn't bothered by the backbiting and machinations of his coworkers. By night, he worked on the club newsletter in his efficiency apartment. Daniel did not have friends other than the forty-three members of his club, and these people he only met at official functions. If you'd seen him walking to the El or the bus stop, hunched, his eyes to the ground, one name you *wouldn't* have conjured was Daniel Boone.

The hall where they met was a drafty place on Clark Street with wide pine floorboards, a stage with an American flag and a podium, folding chairs, and, inexplicably, an old statue of Big Boy holding a plate with a hamburger, fries, and large drink, and leaning in a corner of the hall. Once, the hall had been a meeting place for the Socialist Workers of America.

During one meeting in the middle of winter, Amelia Earhart, an amateur lapidary from Winnetka, was explaining to the group how to set gemstones in rings. She was a woman in her forties who wore too much makeup and kept her black hair in a bun. Gemstones had absolutely no bearing on the actual Amelia Earhart's life or work, but that wasn't necessary. To Daniel's mind, this was one of the most compassionate aspects of the club. One was encouraged to talk, to share with other club members, but what one talked about was an entirely individual matter. It didn't have to have anything to do with your namesake. Some people dealt with their famous names by throwing themselves into imitation; others completely ignored their namesakes. Discussing gemstones was simply Amelia's way of asserting her uniqueness.

"Why are you wasting our time with gemstones?" Einsteen said, jumping from his chair.

Amelia took a soft cloth from her pocket and began intently polishing an agate she'd been displaying to the group. Daniel could see Einsteen had set her back a year or two. How brutish and insensitive. Yes, the discussion had been deadly, but part of the duty of the nearly famous was to listen compassionately and accept. Wasn't this the true difference between the famous and the nearly famous? The famous focused only on themselves and their cult of personality. The nearly famous were more other-directed. This was their strategy, their hope for survival.

Daniel went to the stage and folded his arms around Amelia, who seemed suddenly unaware of her surroundings.

"There, there," Daniel said to her. "Come sit down. That was really a terrific talk. I never realized there were so many varieties of gemstones. Wasn't that a marvelous talk?" Daniel appealed to the other members of the club, who, with the exception of Einsteen, Walt Disnei, and Alfred Hitchkoch, clapped enthusiastically for Amelia. I never should have compromised, Daniel thought. I never should have allowed them membership.

Einsteen should have been ashamed, but bullies never have that kind of self-awareness. Einsteen was tall and gangly, only twenty-three years old, with close-cropped hair. Before coming to Chicago, he'd been a pitcher for the Cubs' minor-league franchise in Charlotte, but had been consistently wild in the strike zone, and had to be let go in the middle of the season. This seemed to be the source of Albert's bitterness, as well as the fact that his name sounded a little ridiculous.

"Why are we meeting at all?" he railed, like some demented union organizer. "Is it to celebrate fame or deny it? Do we want to control fame, our destinies, intertwine them with our namesakes, or wrest control from them?"

"I think that's an individual decision," Daniel answered. "And a personal one. We try to be as nondirective as possible. Really, *club* is a misnomer. It's more of an outreach group."

Disnei and Hitchkoch stood up. Disnei shook his fist at Daniel, and Hitchkoch, red in the face, shouted, "You ponderous windbag! What do you know about fame? What do you know about out-reach? What do you know about real pain? I say we elect a president who knows how to lead, who has a sense of direction."

Dick Nixon, always a jovial fellow, puffed up his cheeks and made the victory sign. "Now let me make one thing perfectly clear," Nixon said in his squeaky nasal voice. He laughed nervously and looked around the room like he expected chuckles or applause. But no one responded and he cleared his throat.

"You see, you see what I mean?" Einsteen said, gesturing at Nixon like he was the manifestation of all that was wrong with the club, with society as a whole.

Nixon said, "I won't be humiliated any longer," and he made his way across the aisle, bumping people's knees, and walked out the door.

"What has this club done for you?" Einsteen said. "Are you better off now than when you joined? Are you famous yet? Isn't that what you really want?"

Daniel could see that Einsteen was getting to some of them. Harry Truman had tears in his eyes. Ernest Hemingway was nod-ding vigorously, shouting out like this was a tent revival, "I hear what you're saying. I'm with you on that one, my man!" "Well, they have a point," said Janis Joplin, barely audible. The four George Washingtons, always a bit of a clique, whispered among themselves.

"Stop picking on Daniel," Shirley Temple said, standing up on her chair. Shirley was perhaps the most namesake-possessed member of the club. Unlike almost everyone else, she tried to dress like her namesake. She was in her thirties, but went in for little-girl frilly dresses and patent-leather shoes. Her hair was black, not brown, but she wore it curled like the real Shirley Temple. Luckily, she didn't try to imitate the real Shirley Temple's voice. This Shirley Temple had a deeper voice, more like Lauren Bacall's. To Daniel, her manner of dress made her seem like she was begging for humiliation. Her behavior was a paradox. Although she dressed like Shirley Temple, she became hysterical if anyone noticed. To Daniel, she seemed to want to exist both inside and outside of a historical context, to be indivisible from Shirley Temple, and yet wholly original. No doubt about it, she was a loon, though there was something endearing about her to Daniel. She cared about the other members of the club, and was the most dedicated besides Daniel, always bringing cookies or banana bread for the members to share at the meetings.

Einsteen ignored her. This all seemed planned to Daniel. Disnei and Hitchkoch seemed rehearsed in what they had to say. Maybe they'd planned a coup from the beginning. "Isn't the real reason we're here," Einsteen said, looking around the room, "that we hate our parents? You're all pathetic. You're the most bewildered group of people I've ever seen. You're not sure if you want fame or nothingness, and it's all your parents' fault. What are you doing here? You're wasting your time. Go home. Visit your parents. Kick them in the shins. Tip them out of their wheelchairs. Take the flowers from their graves. Tell them they've ruined you. They've taken away your lives and given you someone else's expectations." He pointed to the statue of Big Boy, leaning in the corner, as though he was the source of their hopes and dreams.

There was no way to continue after that. The meeting broke up early. Disnei, Hitchkoch, Einsteen, and the rest of their cabal left the meeting en masse, storming in the wake of Nixon. The others stood up awkwardly, stretched as though they needed a break, and fled out into the snow. Daniel stayed around, gathering stray newsletters off the floor and chairs, folding up the seats, and putting them against the wall. Shirley Temple was the only one who stayed to help, and she asked if he wanted company on his walk to the El.

"I think I need to be alone just now," he told Shirley. This was true enough. He needed to sort out his thoughts, but more than this, he was embarrassed to be seen with a grown woman who dressed like that.

Daniel didn't go home right away. He walked east, toward the lake. The snow fell against his back and the wind nudged him along as though leading him to some important meeting. He wore his gray wool overcoat and two scarves, one wrapped around his neck, the other covering his face up to his eyes. He also wore a jaunty wool cap, flat like a beret. Too bad it's not coonskin, he thought bitterly. He walked to Belmont Harbor. The boats were out of the water and the lake had frozen in jagged snow-dusted floes around the piers, except in a few spots where steam rose and dissipated like steady breathing. Signs warned "Danger, No Swimming" and, in Spanish, "Peligro." He focused on one of these spots. The desolation, the anonymity of the spot, the wholeness of the ice—all of these things soothed him, made him feel alone, but powerful in his knowledge that he was alone. Aware that whatever he did was his own choice, not the historical Daniel Boone's, not Fess Parker's, not his parents'. He had free will. He was his own man. He felt reckless, careless. Others had tried on his name before him. One had lived and died. The other, in a series, had been canceled. The name belonged to him now. He felt like *he'd* already lived and died, and nothing could hurt him again.

He dropped down the wall onto the ice of the harbor and started walking. He wasn't sure where he was headed, just out into the lake.

He heard something. A scream. He paused and listened. Now

he just heard the wind, and a little farther off, the traffic on Lake Shore Drive. He wasn't sure if he'd actually heard anything or not. He'd never heard anything like it before. There it came again, tumbling shrilly from some uncertain direction—behind him, ahead, above him. He wasn't even sure if the scream was an external thing; perhaps he was simply tuned into something in his soul, his blood. He'd heard screams before, mostly on TV or in the movies, and the screams of playing children, but he'd never heard a scream to compare with this one. This scream had real terror in it. This scream had frenzy. It exploded with the force of a shattered bottle, angry life trying to contain itself in the body, completely nonverbal, but its message was the same as everyone's message, only more intense: "Notice me!"

Finally, he noticed. He saw something move in one of the boatslips. He wasn't sure what it was, a small metallic-blue blob bobbing up and down in a steaming hole in the ice. An arm raised itself from the blob and the rest of it submerged. Daniel ran toward it. The blob resurfaced and as he drew nearer, Daniel could make out the features of a child, whether a boy or a girl he didn't know. The child had a soaking wool hat pulled down around its ears and a blue snowsuit zipped up to its chin and bright green mittens. The child watched Daniel's progress over the ice. For a moment, the child stopped struggling and hung onto the ledge of ice, watching Daniel almost impassively. Daniel slipped and fell and the child screamed again. Daniel, on his knees, made his way the remaining few yards to the hole. He grabbed the child by the arm and pulled it onto the ice.

The child sputtered and pointed to the surface. Daniel saw a soggy red mitten floating there. He dove in. The water clamped around his chest; his shoulders tightened; his bones seemed to crack; his breath heaved; and when he came back to the surface he let loose a sharp cry. He lost his glasses. He thrashed about, reaching blindly in the water, saw a shadow, reached for it. Dove deeper, holding his breath. He grabbed the child under its arms and started to struggle back to the surface. Ice surrounded him. The opening seemed to have disappeared. He pushed his face against the gray ice. He lunged out, felt his hand reach beyond the ice, found the opening.

On the ice, he tried to resuscitate the child while the other child yelled for help. Daniel, pausing for breath, saw something on the wall above them. Without his glasses, everything looked blurry, but it looked like a man pointing a video camera their way.

"Help!" Daniel yelled.

"Help!" the first child yelled.

The man with the camera waved his arm like Daniel and the child should move closer together. Daniel scooted a bit closer.

"Go get help!" he yelled.

"Help!" the child echoed.

Daniel wasn't sure, but it looked like the man on the wall was giving them the okay sign. The man didn't budge. He went on taping.

Daniel denied he was a hero, claimed he hadn't even thought about what he was doing, but people responded with knowing smiles. In heroism, like alcoholism, denial is the surest sign. Throughout Greater Chicagoland, he became famous, as did the twin brothers he'd saved from an icy death: Little Patrick and Tad Muelhoffer. Little Patrick's survival was in doubt. He'd been underwater for nearly half an hour before Daniel rescued him. The *Sun-Times* established a Little Patrick Muelhoffer Care Fund and ran a daily deathwatch.

On the local news, they showed Daniel's picture and played the theme song from the TV series.

Daniel was flooded with phone calls. Most people praised him; some interviewed him; others seemed confused, bemoaning the fact that his TV series had been canceled, asking after Daniel's sidekick, Mingo. One man from Beverly Shores wondered whether this was merely some elaborate publicity stunt to revive the show. People seemed to need to believe there was some link between Daniel and his namesake. And there was, but what exactly, Daniel couldn't say for sure. This was his life's search, his struggle. This is why he'd established the famous names club in the first place, to discover this link. Maybe the only connection was their common humanity, or maybe they were spiritual twins. The name had a power of its own. It lived and breathed dragon fire. Maybe he couldn't help being a hero with such a name.

A few people who called reacted hostilely, as though they had somehow been personally diminished by his heroism. One man sounded a lot like Richard Nixon.

"I bet you think you're the cat's pajamas," said the voice.

"Dick, Dick, is that you?"

"You're dead meat, Boone," Nixon said, and hung up.

Daniel didn't have to wait long to find how the other members of the club reacted to his fame. At the next meeting, no one showed up except for Shirley, sitting alone in a folding chair, holding banana bread on her lap.

"Where is everybody?" he asked.

"They're not coming," Shirley said. "They've formed their own club with Einsteen. But we can still meet, can't we, Daniel?"

How pathetic she looked, but she was just a reflection of himself, his own desperate need for affirmation. He ran from the hall. Although he lived three miles away, he ran home through slush and puddles. Exhausted, he collapsed on his cot. What was he? A flower or a weed? Fool's gold?

He didn't want this. His friends had deserted him and none of it was his fault. He never asked to be a hero. What was he supposed to have done, let the children drown?

He fumbled for the Chicago directory. Paging furiously through it, he tried to find a name that suited him better, something that wasn't famous. Yes, that was it. He'd change his name. But he didn't want to duplicate *anyone's* name, not even someone obscure. He tossed the phone book aside. It slammed down on the floor. Daniel moved his lips. He picked up the phone book again and slammed it down. What did it sound like? *Phzrok.* No, that wasn't it. There wasn't any way to spell it. Again, he slammed down the phone book. That crashing sound, whatever it was, would be his first name from now on. It was a name that encompassed all the names in the Chicago phone directory and none of them. It was like a Zen koan, a name that could not be spoken, but only intuited. His last name would be the initial *D*. What it stood for would always be his secret, like a mantra. That way he could change it, add a letter, take one away, if ever he heard a name that even *sounded* like his.

He wondered if he could *ever* change who he was. Self-actualization in its various forms—religion, clubs, charities, civic organizations, bowling leagues, lotto, rotisserie baseball—all of it was nothing more than government propaganda or the brainchild of a clever P.R. firm to keep people quiet, to make them feel like winners.

His next task was to murder his parents. It all began and ended with them. Einsteen had been right all along. Once they were gone, he was free to be whomever he wanted.

His parents, Walsh and Muriel Boone, lived in Downers Grove, a short train ride from the city. Perhaps Daniel had always hated his parents—he wasn't sure. He hadn't gone through the typical teenage rebellion, had always obeyed them, even admired them in a distant and subtle way. His mother seemed to be immune to the usual self-doubts. Not that she'd had an easy life. Disagreeable things had crossed her path. She'd grown up during the Depression. Her first child had died at birth. Walsh Boone had been paralyzed from the waist down in a car accident ten years ago, and Muriel had to find employment then for the first time in her life. Muriel had had to battle back from illness, too, breast cancer three years before. Yet she didn't complain, not a peep.

His father rarely spoke, at least since his accident, and seemed eternally joyless. He spent most of his days in his room with the TV on, and rarely ventured outside. Most of the neighbors seemed to think that Daniel's mother lived alone.

Still, Daniel thought he'd gotten along with both of them well enough until now, but maybe that was just a ruse. It seemed that they'd always had it in for him; they must have, since they'd given him such a name.

"Daniel," his mother said, greeting him at the door. "What a surprise." She called into the darkness of the living room. "Look who it is, Walsh. Our son, the hero."

His dad wheeled over and looked at him bitterly, then wheeled around and positioned himself in front of the coffee table as if he were going to defend it. Maybe, Daniel thought, he has some inkling of why I've come.

"We're busting our buttons," said Daniel's mom.

The day after he'd saved the lives of the Muelhoffer twins, she'd called and said the same things.

Daniel stepped inside and said, "By the way, my name's not Daniel anymore."

"You look like Daniel," said his mother. "Come on, take a load off. Want a beer? A hero deserves a beer. Walsh, you want a beer? I don't think you two ever had a beer together."

Daniel's father leaned over completely to one side in his wheelchair and gave him a Sidney Greenstreet kind of look: wily, condescending, and amused. He seemed to be thinking, You gutless wonder. How'd you ever get to be a hero?

Maybe he'd just kill his father, Daniel thought, and leave his mother alone. Daniel sat down on the couch, next to his parents' miniature French poodle, Jocko. His mother went to the kitchen for the beers. "You want to see the garage?" his mother yelled from the kitchen.

"Why?" Daniel said.

"I don't know," she said. "It's been awhile. I thought you might like to see it again."

"Want to see your old room?" she asked, when she reentered the living room. She handed him a beer.

"No thanks."

"There's Jocko!" said his mother, pointing to the ancient dog, who hadn't awakened yet.

"There's Daniel, the hero!" she added to his father in the same pleased tone.

"My name's not Daniel anymore," said Daniel. "You have a phone book?"

His dad jerked his thumb to the coffee table.

"That's Downers Grove. Do you have a Chicago directory?"

"In the bedroom," said his mother. "Is there someone you need to reach?" She looked at her husband and said, "He probably needs to wear a beeper these days." Daniel's dad sniffed.

Daniel went to the bedroom and found the Chicago directory on the bedside table. His dad's reading glasses lay on top of the book, and a yellow card. The card read, "We've been trying to get in touch with you for days. You must call us within forty-eight hours to claim your prize. 1-800-323-5471." Daniel brushed the glasses onto the floor. He stuck the yellow card in the middle of the phone book. He thought it added another dimension to his name. In the living room, he pulled back a bit of the rug and slammed the phone book down beside his dad's chair. Jocko woke up and started yapping at him from the couch, running up to the edge, retreating to the cushions, and running to the edge again.

"That's my new name," he told his folks. They looked at Jocko as though the dog had uttered it.

"What is?" said his mother, looking at his dad. "Hush, Jocko," she said.

Daniel picked up the book again and slammed it down. The dog jumped off the couch and growled at Daniel. "The last name's D," Daniel said.

"What's wrong with Daniel?" his mother said, weakly. "It's a lovely name."

"I didn't get to choose it," he said.

"Now look here, Daniel," his dad said.

"Don't call me that," Daniel snarled, bending down and getting close to his dad's face. He picked up the phone book and placed it across his dad's arm.

"What am I supposed to do with this?" he said.

"Daniel," his mother said, coming up behind him. Daniel whirled and gave her the phone book. She backed up and dropped the phone book, a stricken look on her face. The three of them looked at the fallen directory as though something fragile and valuable lay in pieces at their feet.

Daniel brushed a hand through his hair. He pointed to the frenzied dog at his feet and yelled, "Why did you call that dog Jocko?"

"We liked the name," said his mother.

"Would you have called me Jocko, too? Was that a choice for me?"

"Don't be silly," she said. "Jocko's a dog. You're a boy. We named you after your father's great-uncle Daniel."

"What?" Daniel stared at the phone book. Now was the part where he was going to get up and tip his father out of his wheelchair. When asked why, he'd reply by strangling his parents, first his mother and then his dad. But things had changed. He couldn't move.

His mother picked up the phone book and set it on the coffee table.

"Your dad's uncle Daniel," she said. "Daniel Boone. Wasn't he a chiropodist?"

"A lawyer," his dad muttered.

"I thought he was a chiropodist."

"For God's sake, he was a lawyer. You think I don't know what my own uncle did for a living?"

"Who was the chiropodist?"

"His name was Daniel Boone?" Daniel asked.

His mother nodded. "I remember the sign plain as day. Daniel Boone, Chiropodist."

"Lawyer!" his dad screamed.

"You mean I was named after Daniel Boone, the lawyer/chiropodist, and not the pioneer? Why didn't you ever tell me?" Daniel asked.

His dad shrugged. "We never told you you were adopted either," and he wheeled off down the hall to his room.

A great burden had been lifted from Daniel. True, now he was even more uncertain who he was, but in a good way. He was no longer the son of Walsh and Muriel Boone, at least not by blood, and he'd been named after a man with a profession—whether the law or feet, it didn't matter—not after a pioneer as he'd always thought. The name was the same, but now he felt no connection at all to the famous Daniel Boone. He felt free, like someone who'd been released from a werewolf's curse.

He threw himself into his job at Social Security and was soon promoted. Everyone around him noticed the change, even in his bearing. He lost the stoop in his shoulders. He got rid of the beard. His chin reasserted itself.

Every day after work, he left flowers at the hospital for Little Patrick Muelhoffer, who was still comatose after seven months, and didn't even know he was famous. The *Sun-Times* eventually became bored with Little Patrick's deathwatch. And people who'd sent in contributions were demanding refunds, according to Patrick's mother, whom Daniel saw at the hospital every day.

One day after visiting the hospital, he was walking back to his car when he heard a familiar voice call him. He turned around and saw a young woman in jeans and a T-shirt running after him. Her black hair was cut in a short boyish style. For a moment, he thought it was Demi Moore.

"Daniel. Daniel Boone."

"Shirley Temple! Is that you? What happened to you?" He'd never seen her before without her Shirley Temple outfit.

"Oh this," she said, blushing. "Therapy. Look, I don't even wear patent-leather shoes anymore," and she pointed to her shoes. "How about you, Daniel? How's life been treating you?"

"Great," he said. "I found out I was adopted."

Shirley looked a little bewildered, but nodded and said, "I'm really thrilled for you."

Before this, Daniel had always wanted to flee from Shirley, but now he took his time, and before they were through talking, they'd made a date to meet again.

Their courtship was not easy. It's hard enough to reinvent yourself; it's murder to do it in tandem. Sometimes, Daniel saw some of the old Shirley in her, especially when she started drinking and wanted to sing. And sometimes, Daniel had moments of terror in the middle of the night—he'd awaken with his feet tingling madly, as though his uncle, the possible chiropodist, was operating on them. Of course, the two of them took out their moments of uncertainty on each other, and even broke everything off once, refusing ever to speak each other's name again. But that passed, too.

They married and had a child. They named him Pat, after Little Patrick Muelhoffer. They knew the name would be a burden for young Pat Boone, that everyone would expect him to be wholesome, drink milk, and be a good Christian family man. On the other hand, that wasn't all bad. The world has expectations, whether you're nearly famous or not. Best to impress this on young Pat early. And yet things wouldn't be as rough for him as they had been for his mother and father. Like the historical Daniel Boone blazing a trail through this country, inventing it and being invented by it, Pat's father had blazed a trail for the rights of the nearly famous. The baton was now in the hands of Einsteen, who had turned into a capable lobbyist for the nearly famous and the *nearly* nearly famous, like himself. All over the country now, the nearly famous were making names for themselves.

So the future looked bright for young Pat Boone. He was a lucky child, and his parents told him this every day. They peered into his face when he was a newborn, trying to imagine him grown, wondering who he resembled. He stared back without recognition.

INDEPENDENCE BOULEVARD

LD's IN TOWN, OR MAYBE HE'S NOT. Maybe he's calling from Nebraska and just pretending he's in some phone booth in a convenience store parking lot near the coliseum. His voice sounds like LD's: a hair-trigger laugh inside him, a little high, a little hyper. He says, "You want to play?"

"I'll kick your butt," I say.

"I'll whup your ass," he replies, our little ritual.

"You near the old coliseum or the new one?"

He laughs. "I don't know. It looks like something that McDonald's used to package Big Macs in."

"That's the old coliseum," I say. "Out on Independence. You want directions to the house?"

There's a pause. "Why don't you come meet me?"

He doesn't like to come over because he thinks Mary Elizabeth doesn't like him. It's not that. It's just that women are either in-sanely attracted to LD or repelled by him. There's no in-between. When Mary Elizabeth and I were living together before we got married, LD came over once and insisted on sweeping the kitchen floor. LD can be helpful like that, but Mary Elizabeth was suspi-cious. She called me at work and asked if he was safe. Sure, LD's harmless, I said, but he's given her the creeps ever since.

I haven't heard from LD in three years, and I'd almost thought he'd forgotten about me, or given up on me, but being LD's friend is like belonging to the Mafia. One of these days, you're going to get a call, and you won't be able to pretend it's for somebody else. If you're LD's friend, you're stuck for life.

LD's real name is LD, with no periods in between the letters. He was born in Valparaiso, Indiana. His mother didn't want to name him after his father, Lester Dean Conroe, because she thought he was a jerk, but Lester was a big man in town and she wanted to give her son the advantage of being known as Lester's son. So she named him LD. Of course, in the outside world, people don't know who Lester Dean Conroe is, and they think that LD stands for some-thing. Like Learning Deficient.

It's not that I don't like hanging out with LD. I've known him since college. I'm just not the same person I was fifteen years ago. But LD is. I've matured. I don't like scenes. Like what happened with my answering machine a couple of weeks ago. I was upstairs in my study working on a brochure for a mortgage company when Mary Elizabeth knocked and stepped into the room.

"It's one of your clients. Trish Squires. She says it's urgent."

I probably overreacted. But people like Trish Squires think that every decision they have to make is important. Like a hundred years from now, people are going to care whether *proactive* was the right word choice in a manual for employees of Food Lion on how to deal with espionage attempts. I slammed my fist down on the table and yelled, "Goddamnit! That's why we got a machine. I don't want to hear from these fuckers." The machine was on the table, and when I slammed my fist down, I inadvertently hit the record button. For the next two days, whenever someone called they heard me yelling, "Goddamnit! That's why we got a machine. I don't want to hear from these fuckers."

There were a lot of hang-ups. I might even have lost a couple of clients. It's too soon to tell. So no, I don't like scenes, but with LD, it's like the call of the wild, curiosity, a pact with the devil. I rummage through the closet for my bomber jacket, the one I haven't worn since the last time LD popped into my life, and I'm out of here. History. The big adios. But not before making sure it's okay with Mary Elizabeth. She's planted in front of the TV watching *Stage Door*. Katharine Hepburn is Mary Elizabeth's hero. She says she likes strong women.

"The calla lilies are in bloom," I say, stretching my mouth into a grotesque imitation of Katharine Hepburn.

Mary Elizabeth gives me a look and says, "Yes, did you want some attention?"

"I'm going out," I say. "LD's in town. You mind?"

"You don't need my permission," she says coolly. "I'm not your mother." She says it in the same way my mother says, "I'm your mother."

I peel out of the driveway in my Ford Festiva and head toward Independence Boulevard, where LD's supposedly waiting for me. Driving Independence is no fun and I avoid it when I can. It's a six-lane highway that cuts right through the middle of Charlotte. It used to be four lanes, but the traffic was so heavy they needed a couple of extra lanes. Instead of widening the road, they simply repainted the lanes. So now, on most parts of Independence, you've got about two inches to spare on either side of your car.

I'm wondering what LD and I are going to do this time. We can get pretty juvenile together. Last time, we called up a place called Tommy's Tavern, where the bartender sounded exactly like Popeye. LD and I took turns calling him and asking him to page a friend. The guy kept doing it, no matter how ridiculous the names were. He'd turn around and yell into the room, "Al Coholic! Hey, Al Coholic! Is there an Al Coholic here?"

Finally, he got wise and he and LD started describing sex with each other's mothers.

I'm not saying I'm proud of everything LD and I have done together. I'm just saying I've done it. It's in the past. Like the time LD and I drove to Minneapolis without telling a soul where we were going or how long we'd be gone. The whole point was to disappear, to be unreachable. That was before I knew Mary Elizabeth, before anyone cared whether I could be reached or not. We hitched together, too, got a ride once from a stripper named Jimmie Dawn who dumped us off in Terre Haute, where we were almost arrested for trying to hitch on the on-ramp to the interstate. We stayed overnight in a crummy motel. We'd bought a bunch of decals of pigs in Iowa, and in the morning we stuck them on the inside of the bedside lamp. We ringed the lampshade with pigs in lewd postures. Our tribute to Terre Haute. The pigs weren't visible until you turned on the lamp, and then they cast their shadows on the walls. We imagined a couple on a rendezvous turning on the light and losing their sexual appetite.

I drive into the parking lot of the Circle K by the old coliseum, but I don't see LD, just two cop cars, a large yellow truck, and a Jaguar with four teenagers inside. I park the car by the Jag, and I don't make eye contact with the kids inside. The cops are in the store playing with the Slurpee machine and laughing with the clerk, a man with silver slicked-back hair and a brown mustache. I hate coming to these places, especially at night. Every newscast relates the latest target. Usually, they're far away from my neighborhood, out on Freedom Drive or Billy Graham Parkway, places close to the interstate.

I step out of the car and walk to the entrance of the store. I stand there a second, turn around, and look up at the sky as though I came here for the view. I'm conscious of being neither in nor out of the store, feeling out of place between the teenagers and the cops. There's no sky. It's obscured almost entirely by the giant white coliseum, vacant and useless for the last three years while the city tries to figure out what to do with it. A lot of people want to pre- serve it as a historic landmark.

A couple of years ago, a real historic building, the Hotel Char- lotte, was scheduled for demolition. Instead of simply imploding it, the city made a spectacle out of it. David Copperfield, the magician, was tied up in chains and he had to escape before the building came down on top of him. Thousands of people cheered as one floor after another caved in. I wanted to go, but Mary Elizabeth was disdainful.

One of the pay phones beside me starts to ring, and I turn around and look at it. Behind me, a car door opens and closes and one of the kids approaches. He's dressed like me in a leather jacket, but it looks like it's better leather than mine. He doesn't even look my way. He picks up the phone and holds it to his ear, doesn't say hello, doesn't say a word, just kicks a rock toward one of my tires. I sense him looking at me. I look away. "Hey!" he says, and I shuffle off a foot or so. I don't want to hear whatever's going on. I give up and silently curse LD for bringing me out here for nothing.

"Hey!" he says again, and I look. He's holding the phone out toward me. "It's for you."

I hesitate and he shakes the receiver like I'm wasting his time. So I take it. Next thing I hear is LD's unmistakable laugh on the line.

"Where are you, LD?" I yell. "Goddamn you."

That makes him laugh even harder. The kid beside me doesn't leave. He crowds beside me and listens, as though this phone is his personal property. I wonder what's made me so scared of just standing in a parking lot on a summer night. Sometimes, I don't even realize I'm scared until LD comes along, and then I see how foolish I've become.

LD tells me to turn around and look at the yellow truck parked in the lot. There he is in the cab. He gives me a wave and a stupid grin, his cellular phone crunched between his neck and shoulder. The truck he's in is from the railroad, he tells me. He's delivering it to New Orleans. That's LD's job. He delivers cars and trucks all around the country. It's the perfect job for him. Sometimes, he even gets to drive a luxury car like the Jag those kids are riding in.

I hang up and step into the cab of the truck. He's still chuckling softly, and looking at me with his gleaming, mischievous eyes. The cab is hazy with smoke and LD has a joint in his hand. He offers it to me. I glance at the cops, who are still standing by the Slurpee machine, cracking up. I take a hit and pass it back to LD. First pot I've smoked in three years, since the last time I saw LD.

LD doesn't look quite the same. It's hard to believe he's no longer twenty-two, but his hairline is receding, he's got a potbelly, and his hair is graying. His eyes are large, almost bulging. Mary Elizabeth thinks he looks insane. I don't think so. LD's eyes flash with humor. He's wide open, ready to receive, full of wonder.

"I've never been in a truck before," I tell him. "It's a strange feeling being so high off the road. No pun intended."

"Yeah, kind of like playing three-dimensional chess," he says, and laughs again.

Whatever that means. Just another LD-ism.

"Leave your car here. We'll pick it up later."

LD wheels out of the lot onto Independence, and he doesn't look worried at all as we barrel along, intimidating all the imports in the narrow lanes. First thing he does is phone the kids back in the Circle K parking lot. "This is your dad," he says. "You know what I think of you being out with your hoodlum friends on a school night, don't you? Your mother and I are very disappointed." Then he hangs up and bursts into laughter.

"LD," I say, "watch where you're going."

"Hey!" he yells so suddenly I flinch, thinking we must be about to hit something. He reaches back behind the seat, which is crammed with books and bags stuffed with food and even a couple of paintings, and he rummages. With one hand, he steadies the wheel as we jounce along, and the other one's stretched so far behind him that he's up off the seat. He looks like he's doing some kind of limbo dance, or like a patient whose heart is being jump-started.

"Aha!" he yells, and pulls out an African mask. He laughs and deposits the mask in my lap. This is one ugly mask, with its mouth down-turned, little eye slits, and some kind of funky fur lining its face.

"What do you think?" he says. "It's over a hundred years old. I found it at a little antique store in Elko, Nevada. I only paid twenty-five for it, but I've had it appraised and it's worth several hundred. I was thinking of donating it to a museum, but I want you and Mary Elizabeth to have it."

"Why?" I ask. I'm wondering what made him think of me when he found the mask. LD gives me a look, and I realize my tone makes it sound like I don't appreciate his gift, which I don't. I mean, it looks like something that's got to have some curse attached to it.

"This is great, LD, but maybe you should reconsider. Maybe the best place for this *would* be a museum, where the greatest number of people could enjoy it."

"Oh, I don't know," he says, gazing earnestly ahead of him. Now I know I've been had, but it's too late. "Maybe I'll just take it back to the Goodwill where I bought it. Maybe they'd give me back my quarter for it."

I want to call him an asshole, but that would just give him satisfaction. So I roll down the window and toss the African mask into the weeds. "Hey!" he yells. But then he looks thoughtful and says, "I'd love to see the face of whoever finds that."

There's no surprising LD. I, on the other hand, am surprised by almost everything LD says and does. At the very least, he breaks me out of my routine.

LD pulls off at a country bar called True Grit, a place along Independence that I've passed a hundred times but have never had any desire to go into. It used to be a movie theater, built with funky geodesic crystals of concrete growing out of its walls. Unmistakably sixties.

This isn't LD's style. In college, we made fun of the disco dance lines, and this doesn't seem much different. I ask him why we're stopping here and he looks at me and says, "What? You a snob?"

"Yeah, I'm a snob. This isn't your kind of place either."

"I don't have a *kind* of place," he says. "We don't have to go here, if there's something you're afraid of."

"I'll kick your butt," I say.

"I'll whup your ass," he replies, and we park. I take off my leather jacket and leave it in the cab. If I'm going in here, I don't want to look out of place. So now LD and I are at least partly in the proper uniform. I'm wearing jeans and a T-shirt. He's got on jeans and an Arrow shirt.

It's ten o'clock on a Friday night and there are hardly any cars in the parking lot. These days, I'm usually in bed by eleven.

The old ticket booth has a cow skull and a saddle in it, a picture of the Duke with an eye patch on, one of Sitting Bull, and a sculpture of a wild horse trying to buck its rider off. A chubby guy with long black hair to his shoulders and granny glasses sits behind the old candy counter in the lobby, collecting a three-dollar cover.

"Okay, but only if this is important to you," I tell LD, and shake my head.

"It's not important to me," he says, sounding completely serious, even a little offended. "I just thought it would be different."

The man behind the counter checks my ID. "Hey, it's worth it. It's Laurel Dove," he says, like I should know who that is.

I look at LD. I'm feeling a little cocky now. Maybe it's the joint. Maybe it's the night air. Or the exhaust on Independence Boulevard. Or just LD's company. I feel like I could tell this bouncer to cut his hair and get some new glasses, that John Lennon's dead.

"Yeah, she's not bad," LD says, smiling at the bouncer.

"You know who this is?" I say.

"Laurel Dove isn't her real name," LD says. "She's Croatian."

"A Croatian country-and-western singer?"

"I didn't know she was Croatian," the bouncer says.

"She looks like an ethnic Tanya Tucker," LD tells me. "Maybe that's why she hasn't made it yet."

It's hard to know if he's telling the truth or if he's putting us on. We have this rule that no matter what one of us says, the other has to go along with it. One time, before I knew Mary Elizabeth, LD and I went to a fern bar and we saw this gorgeous woman sitting alone at a table. LD went right up to her and asked if we could sit with her. I never have the guts to do anything like that. She gave him an up-and-down look, then said sure. Before I could say anything, he introduced me as his deaf-and-dumb brother. So I couldn't talk. I just kept rocking back and forth and staring at the woman, bulging my eyes out one moment and then squinting the next. Freaked her out. She excused herself after five minutes.

Past the lobby, the old theater has been gutted and turned into one huge room with stage, dance floor, cheap tables and chairs, pool tables in one corner, a bar in back, and a giant American flag hanging from the ceiling. Over the bar, blocking the projection booth, is the largest deer head I've ever seen.

"What is that, a six-point buck?" I say to the bartender, like I know what a six-point buck is. I've heard people say that before. I figure a six-point buck means that it's a big deer.

The bartender, a young man with broad shoulders and short hair, looks at LD and the two of them smile. "No. . . that's more like a fourteen-point buck, but who's counting?"

"What kind of imports you have?" LD asks the man.

"Chihuahua."

"How about homegrown?" I say, trying to sound relaxed, informal.

"Well, being as how this is a country bar," he says with a thick fake country accent, "we got Bud, Bud Lite, Miller, Miller Lite."

LD buys a couple of Chihuahuas and I buy a couple of Buds and we sit down in the middle of the room. We have our choice of spots. There are about fifty other people here, but they're so spread out that the place feels empty. Two women, one in white jeans, the other in black, are out on the dance floor line-dancing to piped-in music. About half the men are wearing black cowboy hats. There's only one guy in the whole place who's got on a hat that isn't black, and it's tan. Why black? I wonder. I guess no one wants to be the good guy.

"I had a near-death experience," LD tells me suddenly, apropos of nothing.

"A near-death experience?" I say. "You mean you were almost killed? What happened?"

"Not my death, exactly," LD says. "But it could have been mine."

I lean back in my chair and give LD a skeptical look. He laughs, but says, "No, really. I'm serious. It changed me."

"Nothing will ever change you, LD. You're exactly the same as far as I can tell."

LD shakes his head emphatically, takes a swig of beer, and leans in closer to me. "You know, I'm living in Nashville now."

I shrug. "I never know where you're living."

"I was headed home, driving near Opryland, when I came upon an accident. Some kid got thrown a hundred feet from his car. I was the first to reach him. His pupils were dilated and he was bleeding from the mouth." LD takes another swig and wipes his mouth with the back of his hand. "He was shivering and so I did what people do. I took off my jacket and laid it across the guy. When the EMS crew arrived, they asked me what had happened, saw I wasn't really involved, and kind of brushed me off. I left my jacket with the kid. It was all covered with blood anyway, and I didn't think a thing about it. Then later that night, someone knocked on the door. It was a couple of cops, and they asked me if I knew LD Conroe. I told them I *was* LD Conroe. 'Then we have some bad news for you,' one of them said. 'You're dead. You were killed in a car accident this afternoon on the freeway.' It didn't even faze them. What had happened was that I'd left my wallet in my jacket, and I guess the kid who was killed didn't have any other identification on him."

I laugh and shake my head. "That's the difference between us, LD. I wouldn't have gone five feet from the accident before I knew my wallet was missing."

LD doesn't seem interested in that difference in our personalities, but I think about it as he talks on. I'm only half-listening. He talks about how sometimes we think we're making our own choices when we're not, how someone could walk up to us and tell us we're dead, and we'd believe them if they said it with enough authority.

That's what he's thinking about, but me, I'm thinking about pockets. I'm worried about what I just told LD and what it says about me. I keep so much change and junk in my pockets that they make me look like I have grotesque fat deposits. You can hear me walking toward you a mile away. I sound like a one-man band. And it's true, I'm always patting my pockets to see if my goddamned wallet is still there.

"So how are things with you and Mary Elizabeth?" LD asks.

"Fine," I say. "Just great."

"Good," he says.

"Couldn't be better," I say.

"I'm glad," he says.

"We're really happy."

"That's great."

I start to think about what LD told me, that his so-called near-death experience changed him. If that's true, then it's a subtle change, undetectable to the human eye. Maybe it's enough for him to think he's changed. And I'm also wondering how I would have reacted to those cops. Probably not at all. How *do* people change? I wonder.

LD gives me a strange look and laughs. "Did you know that Lincoln was fascinated by the occult?" he says.

I nod. It must be the pot. I can't seem to process anything he's telling me. LD's words float above me. I see Lincoln at a séance. I see him seated at a table with others holding hands, the medium with her eyes closed, saying, "You're dead. You were killed in a car accident this afternoon on Independence."

The room fills up with sound and light and I turn to see Laurel Dove on stage. She's a small dark woman with hair hanging down all the way past her butt. There are five other people in her band, three on guitar, one on keyboards, and one on drums.

"How many of you out there work all the time?" Laurel Dove yells into the microphone. "Let me hear all you hardworking men out there!"

The bartender hollers, but he's the only one.

"I should've known," Laurel Dove says. "It's the gals doing all the hard work. Let me hear it from all you hardworking ladies!"

I look around the room. Everyone's talking at their little tables and ignoring Laurel Dove.

"Well, this song is for you!" she says, as though the whole room exploded when she first asked her question.

The sound system is fuzzy and I can't understand a word of her song. A few couples get up from their tables and wander over to the dance floor.

LD and I don't talk during the song. A woman is going from table to table selling roses from a basket.

The dancers look like they're in some George Romero film, thumbs hooked in their front pockets, watching their feet, blank looks on their faces.

LD and I clap after the song, but we're about the only ones.

Undaunted, Laurel Dove yells, "How many of you out there believe in standing up for what you believe?"

Again, the bartender hollers.

"Well, this is for all of you!" she says, and launches into another unintelligible song. The line dancers go out again, as inexorable as the ocean tide, and I'm starting to get depressed.

"Why did you bring me here?" I ask LD over the noise.

"What?" he yells back.

"Why did you bring me here?"

LD shrugs. I look at Laurel Dove prancing around, her hair flowing behind her. I wonder what's up with LD. This is the kind of place we would have made fun of ten years ago, but LD looks like he's really into the music, tapping his stubby little fingers on his Lone Star Beer coaster. What's with this Laurel Dove? She's the kind of *person* we would have made fun of ten years ago.

"You know, Kevin," LD yells suddenly. "You've changed."

"What do you mean?" I ask, warily.

"You've matured. I mean that in a good way. The well of your experience seems deeper."

I almost laugh at that one. LD can be corny sometimes when he's trying to sound wise.

"How can you tell? We've only been together for an hour."

"I can tell," he says wisely and goes back to his beer and the song Laurel Dove is singing.

When Laurel Dove finishes, she yells out, "How many of you . . . ?" and stops midsentence. "Hey, y'all out there? Any survivors?" She scans the audience with a hand in front of her eyes. "Oh, fuck this," she says, and walks offstage. For a moment, no one reacts, and then her band members slowly unburden themselves of their instruments and follow her. Then the place fills up again with canned country music, and almost everyone jumps up from their tables and rushes to the dance floor.

LD buys a rose from the rose woman.

"What's that for?" I ask.

"You never know when a rose is going to come in handy," he says, and laughs.

"Give me a break," I tell him.

Presently, Laurel Dove emerges from behind the stage and walks toward the bar. She sits down on one of the stools and the bartender brings her a longneck. She takes it and heads our way.

She stops right in front of our table as though she's on a string that LD's pulling. LD hands her the rose and she takes it and smiles. She sits on his lap, puts her arms around his neck, and gives him a kiss. Her hair surrounds them like a curtain.

I've got a buzz. Time has slowed and I'm in that frame of mind where almost anything is acceptable. My head's cocked and my mouth is slightly open and saliva's gathering in the corner for a drool. My voice is a croak, and I'm not sure whether I'm talking or thinking, but a voice in me says, "Yeah, I guess this is truly happening." A woman with hair down to her butt has stepped off the stage, ordered a beer, then made a beeline for our table. She's sat on LD's lap and the two of them are making out. Things like this happen to LD.

I wonder what Mary Elizabeth would think of this. I'd say, "You have to admit. He's got to have something."

While they're making out, I study the place. There's a cactus theme on the walls. My skin feels tingly, like I'm being pricked. I have a cactus in my yard, a big overgrown one that's taken over and choked out some daffodils that Mary Elizabeth planted. If you've ever been pricked by a cactus, you know it's hard to see the little quivers. You just bite them out and swallow, because they're so small. I guess maybe they're still stuck in me, but on the inside where I don't have nerves.

Then I think *I'm* the kind of person we would have made fun of ten years ago, and this depresses the hell out of me.

Laurel Dove scoots off of LD's lap and LD gives a little laugh. His face is smudged with stage makeup.

"Kevin," he says, "I'd like you to meet my wife, Mara Dovnic, a.k.a. Laurel Dove." Then he bursts out laughing and Laurel Dove nods her head at me. "We met in Nashville. I'm her manager, too."

She gives him an adoring look. "LD keeps me sane." She glances out at the dance floor, gives the line dancers a death-ray look, and turns back. "I've never met anyone like him, have you?"

"No," I say, a bit dazed.

Racing signs hang over the pool tables. One says, "Welcome Race Fans." Another reads, "Sunoco Racing Gasoline" and "Champion Performance Proven." I've lived here seven years and I've never been to the Charlotte Motor Speedway. I've also never seen a monster truck crush a row of cars. Or a wrestler careen off the ropes and slam his body on top of his prone opponent's chest.

"LD keeps telling me, 'You've got to meet Kevin. You've got to meet Kevin.' You should hire him as your manager, too."

She and LD laugh and look at me like I'm going to share their laugh, but I'm already on my feet and headed for the door.

In the parking lot, LD catches up with me.

"I don't mind being a fool once in a while, but you must hate me, LD," I tell him.

"What? What are you talking about?" he says.

"I'm always the butt of your jokes."

"What jokes? What are you talking about?"

"You're always making a fool out of me."

"What? Name one time."

"One time! I'll name three. The phone at the convenience store. The African mask. Just now, in there."

LD fumbles for his keys and opens the door to his cab. "I guess you want a ride back to your car," he says quietly.

"I guess," I say, and climb in when he opens the door.

On the road, we're silent. And then LD says, "Kevin, what's your impression of me?"

"What do you mean, impression?"

"What kind of person do you think I am?"

"An asshole," I say.

"Besides that," he says.

I think about it. "You're fun-loving, you're loyal, you're care-free, happy."

"Aha!" he yells like he's got another African mask for me. "You know what? If you asked me to describe myself, I would have used the opposite of all those words, except for fun-loving maybe. And I would have used *your* list to describe you, all except for carefree maybe. You know, you're a little uptight," and he laughs.

We park in the convenience store parking lot and I step down from the cab. The convenience store is empty. There's no one in the parking lot besides us. No Jag. No cop car. No cops inside. I'm glad. I don't know if I could face anyone else tonight. The cops might tell me I'm dead and I'd believe them. Everything that's happened tonight swirls inside me. Welcome Race Fans, I think as I step inside the door. Who cares what the difference is between a fucking fourteen-point buck and a six-point, or whether the calla lilies are in bloom?

LD follows me inside and he says, "Kevin, you all right?"

I'd like to put someone else on for a change. Why not solve the traffic problem by painting eight lines on a two-lane highway? Let the motorists figure it out. Big laugh. Let them crash and burn.

I place a pack of gum on the counter and the man with the silver hair and brown mustache rings me up. He wants to tell me a joke. He says, "Two cops told me this tonight. There was this zebra trying to get into heaven. He went up to Saint Peter and Saint Peter said, 'Are you black or white?' because Saint Peter wanted to know where he should go in heaven. The zebra scratched his head and said, 'I don't know. I never thought about it before.' So Saint Peter said, 'Go ask God. He's over there.' So the zebra went away and came back a little later and said, 'I guess I'm white.' 'Yeah,' said Saint Peter. 'How do you know?' 'Well,' the zebra said. 'God said, "You are what you are," and if I was black he would have said, "You is what you is." ' "

I stare straight at the old coot's dentures and I wonder about all the assumptions he's made in telling me that joke. He assumes I'm going to think it's funny. He assumes I'm a racist. He assumes I'm just like him. I grab the front of his shirt and whisper, "You think that's funny? You think that's funny?"

"Hey," the man says, putting a hand in front of him. "What is this?"

I don't know what this is, I think, and I let go. I'm just standing here and I'm fuming. I'm leaning into the man and the color is rising in my cheeks.

"I don't want no trouble," the man says.

As soon as he says *trouble*, I feel a surge of something in me, something I can't name. It feels strange, but good. It makes my mouth go dry and my thoughts spin. I can't think of what to say, but the man seems to be waiting for me to speak, riveted, his eyes wide open. I don't want to let the man go. He's paying attention to me. He's not smiling. He's looking like there's nothing funny at all.

"I don't want no trouble," I tell him.

"What is this?" he says, his voice shaky.

"You tell me," I say, and I see his hands begin to shake.

He says something about the safe, how he can't get into it, and I'm thinking, That's right. I can't either. I've been in it too long. LD's cruising the candy aisle behind me. "I'll kick your butt," I say, loud enough for LD to hear me.

LD laughs and says, "I'll whup your ass." Our little ritual.

I look between LD and the clerk, and LD's smiling, his eyes bulging like a fanatic.

The clerk opens the cash drawer and tries to hand me some money. Suddenly, I'm awake and sober and I'm looking at the money this guy's got spread on the counter.

"Go on," he says, nodding at the money, his voice a little bolder than before.

"What is this?" LD says, a little laugh caught in his throat as he glances between the clerk and me.

"I don't want no trouble," the clerk tells LD.

"That's right," I tell LD. "Neither of us does."

LD looks surprised, bewildered. It's a new expression and it looks so unnatural on him I almost want to cry.

I notice the man reaching below the counter. I turn and I start running out the door, and I can't see behind me, and I can't speak. The pay phone is ringing. It's still ringing.

THE LAST
CUSTOMER

THE WORLD WAS CRUMBLING TO PIECES and still Allison refused me. Our waiter stood by the table to collect our bill, and
shivered as plaster fell from the ceiling.

"Is there anything else I can get you?" he asked, tears flowing
down his cheeks.

"I think we're fine," I said.

"You didn't ask if *I'd* like anything," said Allison. "You promised me you'd act like a gentleman."

"I *am* a gentleman," I said. "But what could you possibly want
now? This is the end."

A plant in its clay pot toppled off a shelf and busted. A picture
in a golden baroque frame slid off the wall. On the patio, the
wrought-iron tables clattered. Fissures appeared in the restaurant's tiles.

"Didn't you hear what I said, Allison?" I shouted. "You never listen to me."

"I just want to take another look at the menu," she said. "That's no reason to get defensive."

I watched Allison pore over the menu like a translator scrutinizing an undecipherable text. Just a week earlier, we'd gone to the Paris Cafe, and when the waitress had asked if we were ready to order, Allison said yes she was. The waitress had taken out her notepad and stood poised with her pencil, but then Allison had started rattling off all sorts of questions. Was the tuna salad fresh? And by fresh she didn't mean, was it made last night? What about the Crab St. Jacques? Could it be trusted? After all, this wasn't exactly a Crab St. Jacques kind of establishment. Finally, I couldn't stand her babbling any longer and told her to make up her mind. Didn't she see the waitress had other customers? Why did she always act so selfishly?

"There's a big difference between selfishness and thoroughness," she had told me. "I've learned to be more discerning since I met you, Kenneth."

"Take as long as you wish, mademoiselle," the waitress had told us cheerfully in a French accent. "We're really not too busy this time of year," she had added.

Actually, the place had been packed, and our waitress's various customers were clamoring for her attention. One man had held his coffee cup over his head and rapped it with his knuckles. Another man had waved his wallet around like a flare, but our waitress had paid no attention to them. I'd marveled at how calm she stayed in the midst of this, as though we were the last customers who existed, and the fate of the world hinged on what we ordered.

Neither Allison nor I would have done well in the restaurant business. Allison looked at me smugly and folded her menu.

"You see," she had told me. "Waitresses are trained to wait. With you, it's always a matter of life and death."

The waiter we had now was a completely different story. I could tell he was dying to escape. The guy's knees were shaking and his face was completely pale, but he stood by us anyway. He was probably waiting for his lousy tip.

A ceiling fan crashed to the floor and exploded in shards of wood, followed by half the ceiling, which collapsed around us. A choking cloud of white dust rose up. The waiter held a handkerchief over his mouth and coughed.

"Maybe we should leave him alone," I told Allison. "He might want to go to church or visit with his loved ones."

"All I want is some ice cream," said Allison in an exaggerated tone. "You're making it into such a big deal."

"The world doesn't end every day," I said, taking the menu out of her hands.

"Now you're being too dramatic, Kenneth," she said.

A pipe burst in one of the walls and sent water steaming and gushing everywhere.

"We *are* out of ice cream," said the waiter. "And I'm not particularly religious, though I was raised a Catholic."

"We're not interested in your personal life," I said.

"It seems so sad," Allison said, "not to have ice cream when you really want it. I don't mind a little deprivation, I really don't, but ice cream is one of those things that should always be around at times like this. It's so soothing, don't you think so?"

Allison reached out and gave me a little tap on the hand with her fingernail, and a searching look. It was that look that got me. Oh, how manipulative she was, always bribing me with her affection. I started to pull my hand away, but then she added, "Remember the gelato we shared in Capri?" She gave me a wry little smile to remind me. But of course I remembered.

I paid the waiter and he left, counting the money shamelessly to see if we'd left him a tip. As he rang up the bill, a tremor shook the restaurant and a section of wall collapsed on him. I laughed, relieved by the moment's diversion, but then I turned to Allison and saw she wasn't smiling.

"What have I done now?" I asked.

"You promised me you'd stop creating scenes," she said.

"Scenes? What scenes?"

"Lower your voice," Allison said quietly. "You're making a scene right now."

I ran my finger through the condensation on my water glass. The heat was starting to get to me. I took a sip of water and my favorite sports jacket, which was draped on the back of my chair, caught fire. I doused it and threw it on the floor.

"It's no use, Kenneth," she said. "You're blind. No amount of explanation is going to make things better."

"Tell me," I said, wearily playing with my fork. "Why do our worst arguments always happen when we eat out?"

Allison looked at me sadly and said, "I think they're just more noticeable then, not any worse."

One by one, the folded linen napkins at the empty tables around us burst into flames and fizzled into the blackened atmosphere.

We stood and I helped Allison with her coat.

"How do I look?" she said, dabbing at her eyes.

"Your hair's a bit mussed up," I said.

She patted her hair. "What about my mascara? Is it running?"

Allison's face paled as a torso flew by. "How about my lipstick?"

"For God's sake," I said, jumping around her. "We're going to die. Stop worrying about appearances. What about me?"

"You look fine, Kenneth," she said, dabbing at a smudge on my cheek with a finger. "Now you *promised* you wouldn't create a scene."

We walked outside. I looked back and saw a block of concrete slice through the middle of our table. The remaining walls and ceiling collapsed into a smoking heap.

"How much did you leave him?" Allison asked.

"Fifteen percent," I said. "But I don't think it matters much now."

"The service was good," she said. "You should always leave twenty when it's good."

"Forget about these social conventions," I said.

"Social conventions?" she said. "What do you want to replace them with? Doggie conventions? Rat manners? What about human dignity?"

"What about it?" I said, grabbing her by the shoulders.

"You sicken me," she said. "Your promises mean nothing to you."

"What about your promise?" I said.

"What promise?"

"You said you'd marry me if I was the last man on earth."

"So?"

"I'm the last man."

"Take a walk, last man."

And suddenly it was over. The land on which we stood ripped free from the rest of the world and floated into space. But we didn't die because some remnants of the earth's atmosphere still clung to our small asteroid, about the size of a city block. I held onto Allison as we floated around our personal planet. Presently, I saw the rest of the world explode.

"Let me go!" shouted Allison, who still did not grasp the seriousness of the situation.

"Hold me," I said.

Instead, Allison let go. She swung her pocketbook in front of her and glared at me as she spun away, defiant even in the absence of gravity.

"Allison, don't leave!" I shouted, but she gave me a quizzical look, put a hand to her ear, and tumbled out of sight.

Later, kicking among the rubble, I found a giant sign that read, *IS CAFE.* I looked at the sign for a long time, trying to figure out what it meant. "Is Cafe?" I said aloud.

"Oui, monsieur," someone said.

Startled, I turned around. In the midst of the rubble, a small section of Formica counter poked out, and behind it stood a waitress. She seemed somehow familiar. She held a pot of black coffee in her hand. In back, a fancy chrome machine lay on its side, all busted up, ice cream leaking from its spout. Beside it was a blackboard with specials listed, but most had been scratched out, including the Crab St. Jacques, my favorite. Dazed, I walked over to the counter. A single black-and-red barstool remained standing. I gave it a spin and sat down.

THE HOLOCAUST
PARTY

"WE'VE INVITED A HOLOCAUST SURVIVOR to our house, Joel," Amy announced, halfway to Edina, like this was some game show and I'd won the grand prize.

"Excuse me," I said. "A what?"

"A Holocaust survivor," she said in that same tone. "My parents thought that since you're, gosh, Jewish, you'd be interested." She had a hard time saying *Jewish*. She'd even asked me once if Jew was a dirty word. I was horrified by her ignorance, but that's all it was. Just ignorance, not malice. I've always believed that people can be educated. Growing up in the Midwest in towns where there weren't many Jews besides my family, I'd learned to be tolerant. I didn't have much choice if I wanted friends. Besides, Amy was intelligent in other ways. We'd met in college. She'd had a double major in drama and French. I'd seen her in most of our school productions—*Sexual Perversity in Chicago, The Pajama Game, The Apartment.* She complained about always being cast as the ingenue. She tried to act cynical, but she really was the ingenue type. She'd been a twirler in high school, and had won a Little Miss pageant. Her parents were rock-bottom conservatives carved out of Midwestern limestone. Her dad belonged to the John Birch Society. Her mom was a homemaker, nasal-spray addict, and retired child abuser. Now Amy worked in Edina at Laura Ashley in the Galleria, selling dresses her mother approved of and dating a news anchor for KARE who wasn't ready for marriage, but liked showing her off at TV station picnics. Still the ingenue.

What I was doing at the time in St. Cloud, I'm not proud of. But after college I needed a job, and landed one through a family connection at Minnesota Biological Services. We handled animals, cats mostly. It was a job.

But I was glad to take breaks from it, so when Amy called and asked if I wanted to go to a Christmas get-together at her family's house, I said sure. I didn't know how to drive so Amy had to pick me up. And it wasn't a short drive either, all the way from St. Cloud to Edina. I didn't care that it was a Christmas party, but what was I supposed to do with a Holocaust survivor? Jump for joy at the prospect of meeting one? Say, "Oh, you shouldn't have. How thoughtful of you"? In my family, this was not a theme one organized a party around.

Or a holiday. I imagined myself in a box beneath the Christmas tree—alone, in the dark, someone coming by and shaking the box next to their ear: "Sounds like a Jew!"

"I wish you'd told me."

"Don't worry, Joel. She's really very nice. She was my kindergarten teacher. She's the sweetest woman in the world. And her story's amazing."

"That's not the point," I said. "I don't invite Catholics to tell you stories of martyrdom."

Snow started falling and the road became patchy. But Amy didn't slow down in that time capsule of hers from the seventies, an old Cadillac her dad had given her, complete with a CB that wasn't hooked up and a defunct eight-track player. The seat belts had been cut off and the blue vinyl seat had slashes across it. Amy drove as though it were the middle of summer, at least seventy miles an hour. I gripped the door handle and pretended I had a brake on my side.

Trees with snow-covered branches arched over the unlit driveway. The house was a Swiss-chalet type, and from the front looked small, not much more than a garage and a peaked roof. But the place went back a ways, sprawling out over the river. Amy's mother greeted us at the door. She was a copy of Amy, aged twenty-five years, with a too-smooth face, tight, pulled-back hair, and a toothy smile. She was dressed in a Laura Ashley flower print with a white lace collar. I didn't trust her because of what Amy had told me about her. She had a habit of knocking Amy around, though rarely now that Amy was no longer a child.

Amy's dad was in the kitchen reading some magazine, the title of which I didn't want to know. *Armageddon Quarterly*, no doubt. But these people seemed pleasant, and offered me punch and Christmas cookies, and we went to sit down in the living room, which looked like something out of an Andy Williams Christmas Special: a fireplace with roaring fire, Christmas stockings, popcorn strings, a tree with presents underneath. Amy's dad looked a little like Andy Williams, except that he was completely bald. He wore an Andy Williams kind of wool sweater, though he didn't sing but glowered. Andy Williams wouldn't have lasted a season if he'd glowered like that. He would have shaken his guests' hands, offered them punch, and stared. His guests would have felt menaced.

Also in the living room was a roly-poly woman in her sixties, the guest of honor. One of the first things I noticed about her was the pewter cross she wore around her neck. As crosses go, it was elaborate, with the curves and flourishes of a family crest, a fleur-de-lis. I hadn't expected the woman to be Christian. Other than this cross, she dressed plainly, in a brown skirt and dull red top that had faded from washing. She was in her stocking feet, and had her legs curled beneath her on the couch.

"You must excuse me," she said when we were introduced. "My feet are frozen solid." Her accent sounded French. The only other Holocaust survivor I'd known was Rose, my great-aunt by marriage. She bleached her hair blonde and spoke with a thick Eastern European accent. The tattoo was visible on her wrist, but this woman had no tattoo.

Amy's mother fiddled with her pulled-back hair and smiled at me from the hallway entrance. Amy's father stood by the fireplace and poked at it, sending sparks up the chimney.

"Amy, honey," her mother said. "Make sure our guests are comfortable. Why don't you bring in more cookies for them?"

"Sure, Mom," said Amy, bounding into the kitchen as though overjoyed with the task. You never would have known these two had problems.

That left me alone, more or less, with the woman, whose name was Mrs. Isabel. Amy's dad didn't count. He stood frozen by the fireplace, holding his poker near the flames but not in them. Mrs. Isabel patted a place on the sofa and smiled up at me like she was my aunt Rose. I sat down with my knees close together and my arms in my lap, and smiled with my mouth closed. It was a meek smile. If my smile had been my fist, I could describe it as a glancing blow.

Amy bounded back into the room with the tray of cookies just at the moment it looked like Mrs. Isabel was going to start to talk to me. I would have said something to her, but of the two topics that came to mind, one was too trivial and the other too immense: the snow and the Holocaust.

Before turning to look at the cookie tray, Mrs. Isabel gave me one last steady look. Her smile had no pretense in it like the smile of Amy's mom. It was the kind of smile that shows joy that other people exist, not only oneself. I remembered my aunt Rose smiling that way when I visited her, and I wondered if I'd ever smile like that in my life.

Then Mrs. Isabel turned to Amy and darted her finger at a scroll-like cookie. "May I have one of those?" she asked, as if it were an extraordinarily precious object.

"Sure," Amy said. "You can have as many as you want."

"Oh, don't say that!" Mrs. Isabel said, touching Amy's wrist lightly and breaking into a singsong laugh. Amy laughed and I laughed, too. For a moment, I laughed because I wanted to laugh, but then I had to spoil it with my self-consciousness. Thinking again of Mrs. Isabel's smile, I wondered if my laughter was, or ever could be, as genuine as hers. And of course, that brought a little strain to my laugh and a snort came out of my nose. Amy and Mrs. Isabel both glanced at me and I reached for a cookie, the same scroll-like kind as Mrs. Isabel's. It crumbled in my hand.

I must have looked grief-stricken because Amy gave me a sympathetic look, her head slightly tilted, and said, "Don't worry, Joel. It's only a cookie."

I blew a little air through my nose like I thought that was funny and took another cookie.

Amy's mother returned to the room and hovered by her husband at the fireplace. She sniffled slightly and dabbed at her nose with a balled-up tissue. She must have seen me studying her because she looked straight at me and said, "It's a little damp in here, isn't it?"

I gave her my same meek smile, the one that meant I really had no opinions.

Amy set her tray of cookies on the coffee table and sat down beside me. Her dad sat on a stool by the fireplace, the same kind Andy Williams might sing a Christmas song from, and held the poker at his side. Amy's mother sat in a rocker and smiled at me in a way that made me jump up and reach for another cookie. As soon as I sat down again, I took a bite, but felt like I was chewing too loudly, so I held the cookie in my lap and bowed my head. The room was quiet except for popping from the logs in the fire and the creaking of the rocker Amy's mother sat in. Outside, I could hear the buzzing of snowmobiles on the river. For a moment, I thought we were going to say a prayer.

"I've told Joel about your story, Mrs. Isabel," Amy said abruptly. "I think he'd really like to hear it, wouldn't you, Joel?"

I nodded and smiled. Part of me did want to hear it. At least I was more interested than I'd been when Amy had sprung this on me. But I didn't want to hear it in this situation. I was the one in the monkey house, not Mrs. Isabel.

She didn't take much prodding. Amy's asking her to tell the story was just a formality. Telling her story was her reason for being here. Mine was to listen. Maybe if this worked out, we could take it on the road. Bill it as "See the Holocaust Survivor Tell Her Tale! See the Jew React!"

Mrs. Isabel uncurled her feet and sat back, taking us all in and smiling like she was about to tell a Bible story to her Sunday school class.

"I live in Liège," she said. "I am only seventeen when the German invades Belgium, not much younger than you." She had her eyes closed, but I knew that she meant Amy and me. She had a disconcerting habit of speaking in the present tense, as though she weren't an old woman, as though these events were now unfolding around her and her fate might go either way. And the only article she ever used was *the*, which made everything seem absurdly singular.

"By then, the German is spreading himself across Europe, and he needs the workers for the factories because most of the young men are off in our countries, and the German woman is making the war materiel. So he says that all of us between the age sixteen and twenty must go to Germany to work. And like that, I disappear.

"He puts me on the train with hundreds and sends me to Stuttgart, and he puts me in the factory doing metal work—too dangerous, he says, for the German. I hate it, of course, but there's nothing really I can do. I am in his country. He is in mine. My paper says I am the guest worker, but of course I am not the guest. Many of us stay together in a . . ." She fumbled for a word, and opened her eyes, as though one of us owned the word she searched for. "Hotel?" she asked, not pronouncing the *h*. "No, not hotel," she said.

"Barracks," Amy's dad said authoritatively. "That's what you mean."

"Okay," she said. "If you say." She closed her eyes again. "I stay in the barracks and cannot come out at night. The only times I come out is walking from the town to the factory. He doesn't guard me then because where do I go, even with the papers? After all, I am just the stupid Belgian young person and he is arrogant." Mrs. Isabel laughed, and touched her cross.

"He tells me he is paying the wages, but I never see this money because he says I have to pay for the food and . . . barracks, which are so crowded and I am starving most of the time. I work twelve hours a day, every day of the week.

"But of course, I know I am better off than the Jew, who is guarded all of the time. I see him working every day by the side of the road. The German has him there for me, so I can see I am not as miserable as he. I cannot go near, and he is beaten if he stops work. I feel pity for him, but there is nothing I can do. Only once I am able to walk near without being shot. I have nothing with me, but I go up to the old man I see every day. I just want to talk to him."

Mrs. Isabel paused. I realized I had my eyes closed, and opened them now, but Mrs. Isabel hadn't opened hers. In my mind, they were skinny men and boys, all ages, but with the same sunken faces and flimsy patches of hair.

Mrs. Isabel's mouth was open as though a word were stuck there and couldn't be dislodged. Amy's dad stood and replaced the poker by the fireplace. He looked at Mrs. Isabel impassively, then padded across the living room in his burgundy slippers, and went off down the hall. Neither Amy nor Amy's mom paid attention to him, but just getting up in the middle of Mrs. Isabel's story seemed incredibly rude and insensitive to me. A door closed down the hall. Amy and her mother were leaning back in their seats, identical smiles on their lips, like people at a movie who know what comes next and are just dying to tell you.

Mrs. Isabel waved her hand, and the old man beside the road was left behind. I wanted to know what had happened, but of course I couldn't ask. Obviously, she found the memory tough. Had he collapsed? Or stared at her without understanding? Or continued to work without acknowledging her?

Maybe none of these. Maybe she was making it up. She could have just wanted my sympathy.

"One day, my friend Renée and I are working in the field outside of Stuttgart," Mrs. Isabel continued. I closed my eyes again. "We are through with the labor and so we begin to walk home. On the way, we pass the orchard where the apples look red. They are so ripe that they bend down the branches and many have fallen to the ground. My God, apples. It has been so long since I have tasted the fruit. I say to Renée, 'Wouldn't it be nice to have the apple?'

"'No,' she says. She is such a coward. 'We will get into trouble,' she says.

"'Not if we only take a few apples that have fallen already to the ground. Surely, the farmer will not miss these apples.'

"After some time, I am able to convince Renée to follow me, and we run through the orchard picking the fallen apples. We are so happy we don't know what we are doing. We pick up the apple, take a bite, and throw it down. Then we pick up the other. 'This one is too soft,' I say.

"'This one is too firm,' she says, laughing, and hurrying on to the next apple.

"We say we will go home when we are full, before we are missed. We pick up six more apples each to bring with us and start again on our way. Then we hear the voice behind us, the man. He says, 'I hope you are enjoying my apples.'

"We turn around and see the farmer with the rifle pointing at us. He is the old man with the frowning mouth and he instructs us not to throw down the apples we have collected. He says he is going to turn us in to the constable and use the apples for the proof.

"Of course, Renée begins to cry, but the farmer isn't moved. He marches us into town, pointing the gun at us as we carry the apples in our smocks, and Renée begs the farmer for her life the whole way.

"When we reach the police station, I try to tell the constable the side of the story that is ours. I say we are willing to pay for the apples and we took them only because we were starving.

"'Six apples,' I say. "'Only six, twelve in all for the both of us. And they were all fallen, with wormholes.'

"The constable is understanding and he tries to make the farmer see the reason, but he won't. So the constable must do something. He tells us he must make a decision about what will be done with us, and he sends us back to our . . . hotel?"

"Barracks," Amy's mother corrected.

"Or dormitory," Amy said.

I didn't see what difference it made. We all knew it wasn't a hotel.

I heard a toilet flush down the hall, and then Amy's father must have opened the bathroom door because the flushing sound grew louder. He padded back through the living room like an apparition. He was no longer wearing his Andy Williams sweater, but a red flannel Pendleton shirt, a brighter red than his burgundy slippers. He went into the kitchen, where I heard him open the refrigerator, and then he coughed. Amy didn't pay him any attention, but her mother followed his every step with a dark look. She sniffled again and dabbed her nose with her balled-up tissue.

"Later that night," Mrs. Isabel continued, "we approach the guard of our barracks and ask if we may walk. He says we must stay inside, but I say, 'All we want is the short walk. You have our identity papers. After all, we're only two Belgian girls.'

"'You have a point,' he says, and lets us out.

"Of course, we go right away to the train station. We know our chances are not good, but we also know our chances are much worse if we stay. We are sure they will send us to the concentration camp.

"After we are going, we sneak on the train. Renée worries they will catch us, but I tell her I will kill her myself if she starts to cry. We have no money, no identity papers. But I trust God to see us through.

"We spend most of the time on the train trying to avoid the conductor. When he comes, we hide in the bathroom or the dining car. And then we meet the French family who help us by taking away the conductor's attention when he comes near.

"Finally, we reach the border. The German orders everyone out from the train. It is night and we stand outside looking across the border to the lights of a few houses. The train stays there on the German side and the passenger walks one by one through the gate in the fence, where the guard checks their papers. The train starts moving slowly across the border and Renée and I stay back at the end of the line. We have no idea what to do."

Amy's dad returned from the kitchen just then with a beer bottle, holding it by its long neck as if it were some dead game bird. Then he went back to his stool and stared into the fire again. I waited for him to pick up the poker, but he didn't. Instead, he started flicking a finger at his bottle, repeatedly hitting the same high note, which sounded like the warning bell at a railroad crossing.

Mrs. Isabel had been smiling serenely the whole time Amy's dad was going through his routine. He seemed oblivious to the fact that other people were around, much less guests, and he seemed completely unmoved by Mrs. Isabel. I could tell Amy's mom was upset by his banging about, and Amy seemed nervous, eyes darting between her parents, wearing a thin smile. Only Mrs. Isabel seemed unperturbed.

He slowed down the tapping until, finally, the sound grew fainter, and faded completely.

"I notice another gate, closer to the train," Mrs. Isabel continued. "This gate is shut, but there is the space between the fence and the gate, big enough for two skinny girls to squeeze through. Another guard stands by this gate. He is walking back and forth on the Belgian side. So I grab Renée by the arm and we make the way to the gate. When the guard is walking the other direction, Renée sneaks through. Then she calls to the guard as I have told her to do. He approaches her with the smile because she is the very pretty girl and he asks her what trouble she is having. Then while she is talking, I also slip through. But at that moment, the guard turns around and sees me.

"I don't panic. I'm not sure if he does see me slip through the gate. So I think he does not. The large valise sits beside the tracks and I tell him I need assistance.

"'The valise is too big for my sister and me to carry,' I say to him. 'Could you assist us?'

"'Certainly,' he says and he calls over two more guards. The three of them together lift the valise, which is huge, and put it on the train. We thank them for their help and board the train ourselves. I have no idea whose valise that was, but it is lucky it was there.

"In this way, we make our path back to Belgium. When we arrive, we find the friends and the family who help us with the identity papers.

"I pass the war in this same way, working and surviving. Times are difficult and there is never enough of the food. I go to the train station at night and climb to the top of one of the cars carrying the vegetables. I gather as much as possible to bring home. Everything goes fine for a while. One day, I climb to the top of the car with the potatoes. But before I am through, explosions happen from the other trains at the station.

"The whole place becomes crawling with the German. He shines lights all around the station. He fires the guns. And then he spots me on top of the potatoes. He does not shoot—a miracle. He thinks, naturally, I am one of the saboteurs.

"He tells me to climb down. He orders me to say the names of my collaborators. I try to tell him I am stealing the potatoes, not blowing up the trains.

"Of course, he doesn't believe me and he locks me in the box, with only the tiny hole to see and breathe. He promises to shoot me in the morning. The German always does everything quick, but he likes to wait until the morning. I don't know why. Maybe he must start the days cruelly in order to continue this. Maybe it is easier to do this after he has slept and fed himself.

"The whole night I pray. I can see nothing, but I hear the shouts and the running feet and more explosions and the guns. At dawn, I hear the yelling closer and I shout, 'What is it?'

"It is the Allies. They have captured Liège and I am saved."

With that, I opened my eyes, and saw that Mrs. Isabel's eyes were still closed. Then she opened them, smiled, and looked at me. Amy and her mother were also looking at me.

"Isn't that remarkable?" Amy asked.

What could I say? It was remarkable, amazing in fact. I was impressed, but anything I might say seemed trite, though necessary, just as all major events—births, marriages, deaths—need to be attended by words. But before I could say anything, Amy's father spoke up.

"What about Renée?" he said. "You never said what happened to her."

There was hostility in his voice, and I wondered what his problem was. This guy was definitely touched, whacked out. Amy blushed and her mother stared politely at the rug, but Mrs. Isabel hardly seemed to notice.

She shook her head and pointed at the ceiling. "She is killed by the bomb," she said. "We are sitting at the cafe when the air-raid sirens occur. Everyone runs in whatever direction, but as I cross the street, a fat man steps on my toe and breaks it. Renée helps me across the street, but . . . she does not get there."

We were silent, and I thought about Renée begging for her life in the orchard, and the way Mrs. Isabel had portrayed her as silly and innocent and cowardly. I imagined this thin young woman, nineteen or twenty, forever moored to those awful years of the war.

I was startled by Mrs. Isabel's singsong laugh. "This toe is the only thing I am left with from the war. You see, I do not go to the doctor because I do not think it is serious. Then it swells up so big, and the woman whose house I am living in sees it and says, 'My God, we must take you to the doctor.' But by then, it is too late and the doctor must remove the toe. But I know I will survive. My faith in God has seen me through, and why would He let me survive so many bad happenings only to kill me from the broken toe?"

I didn't know. It wasn't a question I could answer, but I thought about it.

Then Amy's dad stood up. He was holding his poker again. "That must have hurt a lot," he said. "I bet it still hurts."

"Roger," Amy's mother said.

"What?" he said. "I'm just saying that losing your goddamn toe would smart."

He placed the poker beside the fireplace and it brushed his beer bottle. The bottle tipped over the fireplace ledge and onto the floor, where it rolled with a clatter to the edge of the rug. Beer foamed out of the bottle.

He stormed out of the living room and out the front door into the snow. He didn't bother to put on any outdoor clothing, not his Andy Williams sweater or an overcoat. All he had on was his red Pendleton shirt, his thin brown slacks, and his burgundy slippers.

Mrs. Isabel and I pretended nothing had happened. She looked in her purse for something, pulled out a pack of gum, and offered me a piece. "The mouth gets so dry," she said, "when I talk so much."

Amy's mother was already in the kitchen, getting something to wipe up the spill with, I assumed. She poked her head around the corner, a roll of paper towels in her hand, and said, "Amy, will you come here a moment?"

"Sure," Amy said, and smiled at me like her father hadn't just gone balmy and run out the front door.

I took a piece of gum from Mrs. Isabel and thanked her. The two of us sat there chewing our gum, looking at the fire, which had started to fade.

"That was an amazing story," I said.

"Yes, life is strange," she said, as though this is what I had remarked on. She didn't seem to be sitting beside me. She still seemed to be back in the war. "I am sure that God is watching over me. This is how I survive."

Then she turned to me and she seemed back in the present. "I am glad though the German never gives me the blood test," she said.

"A blood test?" I said. "Why's that?" I laughed, thinking this might be some kind of joke. What did blood tests have to do with anything?

"My grandfather," she said, "is Jewish. I look Jewish. If the German gives me the blood test, he will know."

"Excuse me?" I said.

"The Jewish blood," she said. "It is thinner than the normal blood."

"Excuse me?" I said, or I think I said it. Maybe I didn't say anything at all. Maybe I just sat back and wondered if I'd heard her correctly.

In any case, she didn't answer me. She just closed her eyes and hummed a note. "Mmm, good gum," she said.

Suddenly, I was afraid of something, but I didn't know what. For some reason, I saw the animals at the lab.

I wondered where Amy was, and why her mother had called her aside. Things were too quiet. I imagined Amy's mother pinning her to the wall, slapping her across the face, saying that her father's outburst was all Amy's fault. It didn't make sense, but that kind of abuse never did.

"Excuse me," I said to Mrs. Isabel. I stood up and walked through the kitchen, but Amy and her mother weren't there. The paper towels sat on the counter.

I found Amy and her mother in the hallway. At first, they didn't see me. They were talking softly, anxiously, but they were separated by a few feet. As far as I could tell, Amy's mom hadn't touched her, had hardly been near her. Then Amy turned and saw me, and

Amy's mom saw me a moment later. Amy's mother smiled and walked toward the bathroom. Amy approached me and took me by the arm.

"Sorry about Dad," she said. "He was in the war, too. He spent it in a Japanese camp in the Philippines."

I only half-heard her. I was still trying to make sense of what Mrs. Isabel had said, how someone who had gone through so much could say something as ignorant as what she had told me, that she could believe this Nazi lie for nearly fifty years.

"Are you all right, Joel?" Amy asked.

"Sure," I said. "I'm just trying to take in Mrs. Isabel's story."

Amy shook her head. "It's amazing, isn't it?"

"Amazing."

"I guess you probably need to head back now," Amy said.

"Early day at work tomorrow," I said. "But thanks for inviting me."

Amy smiled sadly at me. "Okay, I'll be right out. I just want to make sure my mom's all right. She says it's getting harder and harder to live with him."

Amy went off after her mother and I went outside and stood by the car in the snow. I didn't want to say good-bye to Mrs. Isabel and I didn't care if she thought I was rude. Amy's dad stood at the end of the driveway by the mailbox. He was looking out at the road. The snow shifted around him, swirling into a small drift by his feet. Maybe I had judged him harshly. Maybe people are more complicated than simply what they've read, what they've experienced, even what they've survived.

I saw a woman once on TV who had shot her own children, shot them—only no one knew at the time that she had done it. She'd shot herself in the wrist, too, to cover up the crime. But when she talked, she seemed concerned only about her own flesh wound, and talked flippantly about the whole incident, though one of her children was dead, another paralyzed, and another ravaged by a stroke.

What I'd told Amy was a lie. I didn't have to be at work early in the morning because I wasn't going back there again. Even so, I had worked there for six months, and that can never be erased, no matter what. But I know one thing. I'm never going to talk about it.

SAINT OF THE ROOF RATS

THESE PIGEONS AREN'T SYMBOLS OF ANYTHING. They're just pigeons. Roof rats. So what if my wife is pregnant and nesting in a big way, and hates my undeclared war against the pigeons? None of that matters. There's no correlation here. Life isn't that tidy. No one up there is trying to send me a message, even if my dreams *have* been full of flapping wings surrounded by furious light. And if there were a message, what would it be? Some kind of meta-physical blackmail? Touch the pigeons and the kid's born with a defect? Or dead? "Love thy pigeons as thou would love thy own child."

No way, not me.

"What's more important?" Janet asks. "The house or the pigeons?"

"The house," I say without hesitation, shocked that she'd think otherwise. She's shocked as well, angry that I'd value something material over feather and blood. She doesn't speak to me for a day. "I'm not angry, just disappointed," she says.

"They're dirty, filthy," I say. "They carry disease. Their droppings coat the car, the house, the porch."

"I don't want to get into it," she says. "I'm just disappointed, that's all."

"Disappointed? I just can't stand the mess."

"You don't really want this baby, do you?" she says.

"That's not true," I say, but whatever Janet *says* is true becomes true, whether I believe it or not. She has an almost Midas-like ability to turn opinion into truth, fabrications into givens.

She leaves me pondering her accusation. I'm looking out the back door. Outside, the sparrows are taking a dust bath on the bare spot of our lawn. Actually, that *is* our lawn. We have two dogs who've trampled the grass beyond salvation. I gave up on a lawn a long time ago. But I'm not about to give up on the rest of the house.

So now I skulk around in secret, like this is some habit, some filthy blood lust, like I'm a serial killer, not merely a neurotic homeowner.

First, they take over the eaves. My ladder isn't tall enough to reach them, so I take to throwing pebbles at them from the driveway. Usually, they flap away at the motion of my arm. As they fly, they make a sound like the blades of a helicopter as it slows down— a hollow sound—like Curly of the Three Stooges as he spins in circles on the floor and mindlessly whoops.

I especially hate their dumb voices in the morning. Janet says it's soothing, like doves, but there's something infuriating in that modulated gurgling of theirs.

One large rock skitters across the eaves where a pigeon had been moments before. It makes an arc across the slant of the roof, bounces off the gutter, and lands smack in the middle of the hood of my car. The rock makes a noticeable dent. I look across the driveway at the roof of my neighbor's house. The same pigeon is strutting on the peak of the roof, making Curly sounds.

I've decided this is too big a job for me to handle alone, so I hire a carpenter to cover the eaves with lattice. He tells me it'll be cheaper if I paint the lattice myself. I spend an entire afternoon painting my lattice slate gray, the same color as my house. As I paint, I look up at the eaves, where the cocky bastards are doing their Buckingham Palace Changing of the Guard routine—marching from one end of the eaves to the other. "Soon, my pretties," I say in my best Wicked Witch of the West imitation (which is none too good). If I had flying monkeys, now would be the time to unleash them into the skies.

But all I have is my carpenter, Scott, who arrives one day to install the lattice, climbs the ladder, and announces that he's found some hatchlings there. "There weren't even any eggs there a few days ago," he says.

I'm not into boarding up living creatures, Cask of Amontillado-style. I'm not after revenge, merely the American Dream.

Another month goes by, and this time Scott succeeds in putting up the lattice. I figure I've solved my problem.

The pigeons can't believe they've been evicted. My eaves were their five-star hotel. At the height of the pigeon season, there were well over a dozen of them up there. Now they've been reduced to six malingerers who refuse to give up, who spend their days walking the gutters in front of the lattice. This in itself presents a problem. The pigeons either poop in the gutter or, more frequently, over the side, onto my car, a red Mazda 323. After a week, the car is spotted with pigeon dung and feathers.

"Poor pigeons," Janet says one night as we pull out of the driveway to go to a restaurant. "You've taken away their home." Janet rubs her abdomen as she says this. She's beginning to show and is wearing a loose-fitting blouse. We're at the four-month mark now. At first, the doctor was worried about a miscarriage, but Janet quit her job and spent a couple of weeks lying down, and now we've passed that dangerous first trimester. We're going out to cautiously celebrate this milestone.

I could leave her remark alone, but it burrows into me. "Either I take away their home or they take away ours."

"You care more about those pigeons than you do our baby."

That does it, and we wind up getting into an argument and turning around halfway. At home, I sulk in my favorite chair while eating a bowl of Oat Bran Options. I'm furious at Janet. All sorts of thoughts go through my mind. Abandoning Janet and the baby. Blowing the pigeons away with a shotgun. Munch, munch.

The pigeons, instead of giving up, simply move their base of operations from the sides of my house to the front and back. In the front, they've taken to roosting on a ledge above the two pillars by the entrance. In the back, there's actually a little cubby above the door that they can fly into and out of. It's been there ever since we moved in, and Janet and I have no idea why. It was closed off for a while, but when we had our gutters put on, the workmen had to tear down the facia board in front of it.

The neighbors, never short on good gossip, have taken to discussing my pigeon problem among themselves. No one else is haunted by pigeons, just me. Ella, across the street, sits on her porch all day with her pit bull, Precious. Ella is shaped like Buddha, and spends most of the day and night on that porch, so she has had plenty of time to consider my problem. One day, I visit with her over her chain-link while Precious growls and she tries to quiet him by saying, "Hush now, Precious."

"You might could try one of them plastic owls to scare them fellers away," she tells me.

I imagine a big inflatable owl hanging from my rafters. Knowing my pigeons, they'd probably treat it like a sex doll. Anyway, I can't imagine having a faux owl greeting guests as they enter my door. That would be as bad as flamingos.

"You might could shoot them," she suggests. "I'll borrow you my Smith and Wesson."

"I don't think I could do it," I say.

"That's right tender-hearted of you," she says. "We had us some pigeons once. They nested over there by Pedro and his donkey." She points to the concrete statue that I've always considered an eyesore. "Precious ate every last one of them." Then she gives me a big evil laugh.

Inside, our house has taken on the look of a baby shrine. As the due date draws near, Janet and I ready the nursery. We buy a Persian rug made in Chicago. We buy an antique quilt for the wall. A rocker. We have a stroller, a humidifier, a nursery monitor, a car seat, and various stuffed animals. I paint and Janet hangs curtains. When the nursery is finished, we shut it off from our pets, our two dogs and two cats. We hermetically seal it. It's our baby time capsule. The nursery is almost like the preserved room of a dead person. Only this is the opposite case. Maybe I sound cynical or flippant, but I'm not. I've been spending almost as much time on the baby shrine as Janet. It was my idea to buy the cherry Simmons crib and matching dresser. Janet thought it was too extravagant. The crib has a white lace canopy, which alone cost ninety dollars. We had a choice between buying a fancy crib and sending our child to college, and I wisely chose the crib. I've also had a burglar-alarm system installed in our house, and have called Scott over to see how much a patio out back on our bare lawn would cost. He says a patio would cost sixteen hundred and a deck would only cost sixteen-eighty, so I might as well go with a deck. Janet says it's moot since I blew all our money on the crib and the alarm system to protect the crib. Okay, that's true. Still, it's good to know how much a deck or patio *would* cost if we could afford it. She says, "Relax, stop pacing, you're making me nervous." I say, "Let's go to Target. Don't you need another nursing bra?"

Once in a while, we grab a stuffed animal and coo and cuddle it in front of our dogs, as one book suggested, to get them used to a baby. They think we're crazy and we feel foolish, so we don't do this often.

Outside, a pigeon couple takes over the front ledge. The male is dark and the female is white with gray spots. The male seems to have the job of nest-building, and he's fast about it, too. Every day he builds a nest and every day I climb my ladder and take it down. "Can't you get the message?" I yell at them as they fly off going "Whoop, whoop, whoop."

At various points in the day, I sigh and say, "I wish I could get rid of those pigeons."

If Janet is near, she says, "Don't tell me what you're doing. I don't want to know."

The black-and-white couple are stubborn. They're wearing me out. Janet says hello to them every time we leave the house. I keep a big stick by the front porch. Every time I leave or enter the house, I grab the stick and go WHACK on the front pillar. The pigeons flap up to the roof, strut until I've gone inside, and then settle back on their ledge. I set bricks up on end around the ledge, thinking the pigeons won't have room for a nest now. They don't need one. I've created a nice little fort for them. The white pigeon pokes her head from behind the bricks when I open the front door.

It happens one day as I knew it would. Right before Lamaze class, I discover a warm egg behind the bricks. A pigeon abortion. The dogs watch as I sail it over the back fence. So does Janet, who has sneaked up behind me. "What are you *doing*?" she yells. "How can you be so mean?"

"It's not as though I'm killing a live pigeon," I try to reason. "Just some yolk."

If we had been headed anywhere else besides Lamaze, we'd have canceled. But we can't cancel Lamaze, so I drive her silently to class.

Vicki, our instructor, says that during labor, especially transition, the woman might lash out, say things she doesn't mean. I don't have to wait that long. During class, Janet breathes fiercely at me with short shallow breaths using the upper portion of her lungs, just as she's been instructed. "Hee hee hee," she breathes. She's reclining on two pillows against the wall. Vicki says, "Coaches, make sure she's relaxed. Look for trouble spots and touch them, but don't say 'Relax,' say 'Release' instead. That's a more relaxing word."

All I see are trouble spots. I don't dare touch them.

"Pigeon killer," Janet says between breaths. "Hee hee hee. Baby killer. Hee hee hee. How are you going to treat the baby when it's born?"

"Heave it over the fence if it poops on the car," I say, matter-of-factly. In the best of moods, Janet is merely tolerant of my jokes. When she's angry, my jokes infuriate her, but sometimes I just can't resist.

The couple closest to us glances our way. His name is Nestor and her name is Shirley. Nestor works for the government and she works for an insurance company. At the first class, we had to introduce them and they introduced us. It felt like *The Newlywed Game.* Nestor and Shirley are working harmoniously, he's rubbing her trouble spots, she's breathing and smiling at him. Since I can't touch Janet, I hold up fingers for her. "Four, three, two, one, now *deep* breath."

"You creep," she says, throwing Nestor and Shirley off their count. I believe we're in transition, but nothing's being born.

Despite the mounting evidence, I still refuse to believe that someone's trying to give me a message. Forget the fact that the pigeons won't go away, that they haunt my house no matter what I try. If I were an ancient Greek, okay. Maybe then I'd believe Zeus had transformed himself into a pigeon to teach me a lesson.

I know I should just give in. I know that the pigeons are too dumb to lose, too ignorant to realize they've tried unsuccessfully to build a nest in the same spot a thousand times. I know that these pigeons are breaking up my marriage, that Janet is growing more distant and shutting me out. She won't even tell me the baby names she likes. She claims I'm too fickle, that I like one name one day and hate it the next. But that's not the real reason. It's the pigeons. They're turning her against me. And what about Nestor and Shirley? No one's really as lovey-dovey as they are. No one can really be named Nestor.

I should give in, but I can't. This is *my* house.

I go to the hardware store and buy nine feet of one-by-six board and nail it over the cubby in back. There are holes in the side of the cubby, too, so I nail some scrap plywood over the openings.

Suddenly, it stops. The pigeons in front disappear. The pigeons in back disappear. The pigeons along the gutters . . . gone. Each day when I leave, I glance up at the bricks, but the white bird, whom I've named Shirley (and her companion, Nestor) doesn't poke her head out. In the morning, I no longer hear the dumb whoops as they fly from one roof to another. I listen over the sounds of the air conditioner in the morning, but nothing. I wake earlier than usual, feel restless, take a shower, have a cup of coffee, call in sick to work, return to bed. I feel listless all day, though not really sick. The symptoms are nothing I can identify, the illness nothing I can name. The next day, I wash and wax my car. It's sparkling clean. I stand back and admire it. I go inside, glancing up at the row of bricks on the ledge.

Janet's sitting in her rocker, rubbing her stomach and looking down at it with a troubled expression. "She's been awfully quiet today," she says.

I take her hand and rub the back of her neck. "How long?" I ask.

"Twenty-four hours at least."

"Maybe we should call the doctor."

"No, not yet."

I imagine the cord wrapped around the baby's neck, or that there's something wrong with the placenta.

"Can I get you something?"

"Maybe some water."

I go into the kitchen, open the refrigerator, and pour the water from our pitcher with the water filter. (My idea early on so the baby wouldn't be harmed by hidden poisons. But what kind of filter can protect a child from a pigeon curse?)

As I'm pouring, I hear something from outside. It sounds like chirping. I put down the glass of water and hurry onto the back porch. I look up at the closed-off cubbyhole. The chirping is coming from inside.

I return with Janet's water and then tell her what I've heard.

"I'm not *sure* it's really coming from inside there," I say.

We stand out on the back porch together and listen intently. After a moment, it comes: a chorus of chirps. There must have been eggs in there I didn't see. They must have hatched.

"You better open it up again," Janet says.

It doesn't take long. I only had one nail holding the plywood on anyway.

"I guess I can live with them another month," I say.

"Good boy," Janet says as if I were one of the dogs, and rubs my hair. "Oh my."

"What's wrong?"

"Nothing," she says, smiling. "She just turned over."

Later, I make popcorn and sprinkle it out in back in the bare yard. I don't have birdseed. Sparrows and blackbirds and robins and even a cardinal come down. They dance around the popcorn, swoop down from trees. It's a neighborhood party. I call Janet over to look at the birds, but before she gets to the back door, they fly away as though they've been startled.

"Look at all those birds," she says.

"They were here just a second ago."

"Wow, they sure do love that popcorn."

"Shush," I say. "They *were* here. They just don't like you."

"They don't like *me?*" she says. "I'm their protector. You're the bird killer."

"I'm *not* a bird killer," I say.

"Peep peep peep," she says in a pathetic baby bird voice, and walks away.

As soon as she leaves, the birds slowly return. I want to call her back to look at them all, but it's not really necessary. This show seems to be meant for me. As I'm watching, a pigeon—Shirley, the white one from up front—emerges from the side of the cubbyhole and swoops down in the middle of the other birds. She pecks among the popcorn, cooing.

A PRINTER'S TALE

For Max Childers and Steve Sherrill

A MAN ON MY LAWN IN A WHITE SUIT and a Panama hat is calling me down. He's a little chicken-headed fellow with a bow tie. He's holding a hip flask in one hand and a rolled-up copy of a magazine in another. He's one of the scrawniest fellows I've ever seen and his gray hair hangs to his shoulders.

He looks unsteady on his feet. His legs are spread apart like he's trying to keep balance on a ship, and when he sees me in my window looking down on him, he takes two steps backward like he's been blown by a gale. He raises the rolled-up magazine and yells, "Are you Lawton Pettis?" His voice comes out hoarse.

"Who's there, Lawton?" says Naomi behind me. I turn back to her. She's curled up on the mattress with the sheet twisted around her. On the table beside the bed is a fat blue scented candle and Naomi's crystals. The room still has a bayberry scent to it. There's also a copy of Naomi's first poetry publication, twenty-six of her poems in a national magazine. Except for Naomi on my mattress, the nightstand, and a tiny wooden stool, the room is bare. There aren't any posters on my walls. There's a hole in the plaster where I punched my fist when Naomi wasn't mine. Still, if not for the man screaming on my lawn, I'd think my life complete, and my room the perfect picture of beauty and refinement.

"Are you Lawton Pettis?" the man yells again. "The Lawton Pettis who, until recently, worked for H. H. Porter Printers in Charlotte?"

"Depends if you're from MasterCard or not," I say. "I told you I couldn't pay more than ten dollars a month, so it won't do you any good coming round and harassing me."

The man lets the flask drop to the lawn. He does a little floppy dance in a circle, clutching his side, and I think maybe he's having some kind of attack, but then I see he's laughing silently. He's howling with laughter, only no sound is coming out, and he's squatting in the grass like he's doing some kind of rain dance, his long skinny arms dragging the ground.

Slowly, he straightens up and, still clutching his side, takes short breaths and manages, "That's too funny."

"Go away," I say, and start to close the window, but I only get it halfway down before this little man says in a fierce voice, "Lawton Pettis, I am a creditor. I want your ass in a sling. I want to ruin your life the way you ruined mine."

"Go away!" I yell. The man's crazy. I've never seen him before, and no creditor would act like that.

"Who," he starts, and then a little louder, "WHO or what is the creature called Naomi Thigpen?" That freezes me and I turn back to the window.

"Who is it?" Naomi says. "Is that Roger?"

"No, it's not Roger," I say. "Roger's history, and he's not about to show up on my lawn and tell me he wants my ass in a sling. For God's sake, Roger doesn't even eat meat and he won't wear leather shoes. You think he knows how to throw a punch? You can just forget Roger."

"I was just asking," Naomi says, turning away slightly.

"I'm sorry," I tell her, shielding my face with my hands and scrunching my shoulders like I'm cowering. Maybe I overreacted, but Roger's just a grinning idiot. Once, he told me he'd kissed every inch of Naomi's body. He said it with a tone of wonder. I felt like shoving a leather sandal down his throat, but that wondrous tone stopped me. He said it not to be dirty, but with awe, like he was talking about the Statue of Liberty, and that's how I feel about Naomi, too. Instead of punching him, I felt like putting my hand over my heart. Naomi says I put her on too much of a pedestal, that I don't treat her like a real human being.

But she deserves to be treated differently. That's why I helped her with her poems. At H. H. Porter, they typeset and print some of the most famous magazines in the country. Printing costs are cheaper down here. Sometimes, I used to read the magazines. Sometimes, I made little changes that no one would notice. A period here, a comma there. One of the magazines never made any sense. The poems and stories never had a point. They all just seemed to have been written off the top of somebody's head. So last month, I took all of Naomi's poems in and substituted them for that crap. I had to take out some other stuff, too: a few cartoons and some drama reviews. And then I typed in the computer on the contents page, "A special selection of poetry by Naomi Thigpen." Then, when the magazine was printed, we shipped it off to the distribution warehouse in Atlanta like we always do. Naomi was so excited when I told her I'd submitted her poems and that every one had been accepted for publication. "See," I told her. "You deserve to be put on a pedestal."

"Yoo-hoo!" the man on my lawn yells, cupping his hands around his mouth. "Yoo-hoo!"

"Who are you?" I say.

"Never mind who I am," he says. "Just tell me about this Naomi Thigpen creature."

"Naomi Thigpen," I declare, my voice a war cry, "is my . . ." I have to think for a moment. Naomi, in the meantime, has put on her tie-dyed shirt and jeans, and stands beside me and says, "I'm not anything of yours, Lawton, so shut your mouth before your brain gets permanently behind."

She turns to the man and says, "I'm Naomi Thigpen."

"Ah," says the man, taking off his Panama and dusting the ground with it. "A vision of mediocrity."

"You shut up, you little chicken head," I tell the man, pointing my finger at him. "I'm coming down there right now."

"Don't you dare," Naomi tells me. She belongs to this group called Beyond Strife. She brought me to one of their meetings once. A bunch of doctors, dentists, and teachers. They sit around and jabber about how everyone in the world has to get rid of all the hostility in their personal lives, and then they can get rid of war.

The man unrolls his magazine and starts reading out loud. It's one of Naomi's poems, a favorite of mine. Suddenly, I have a sick feeling. Or is it excitement? Naomi's poetry being read all across the country at this moment. As the man reads, he gestures with his arm like he's reading the Declaration of Independence.

The Plight of the One-Legged Pony

The one-legged pony is dying
and we the people are crying
as sobbing dolphins float like
lazy clouds above.
For they are the truth and

the proof is in the blood
of a dove.

The one-legged pony needs me.
Where should I be, what should I see?
The fate of the little one
resides in my heart. Help.

The one-legged pony must live,
because he is
humanity.
We must be strong and sing
long into the future.

I'm almost in tears when the man gets through reading. I can almost see the poor little pony standing there, leaning against a barn. I touch Naomi's hand, but she pulls away.

The man clutches his side again and starts laughing silently. When he recovers, he gasps, "How did you ever think of such imagery?" Then he turns around and drops his pants. Naomi squeezes my arm near my elbow. She's turned a little pale.

The man picks up his trousers and buckles the belt. "That's one of my earlier poems," Naomi says weakly. "I was kind of surprised it got accepted."

"Accepted!" the man squawks. "Accepted!"

"Don't you appreciate good poetry?" I ask the man.

"Yes!" the man screams, and drops to his knees. Tears squeeze from the corners of his closed eyes, and I think maybe Naomi's poem has caught up with him in a delayed reaction. Still, I don't know why he mooned us.

The man pounds the lawn with his fist and screams, "Yes! I appreciate good poetry. That's why I took the first flight from La Guardia. That's why I want your ass in a sling. I appreciate good poetry. I have killed scores of men and women for love of good poetry." He looks up at us, blinks, and says in a softer voice, "Career-wise."

At the printing plant, I followed the magazine from the paper cutter to the bindery. First, I helped Ed, the paper cutter, stack loose pages on the skids. Then I helped wheel them over to Charvyn, who was working the collator. Charvyn's an old girl who's built like a deluxe freezer and lives for her Harley-Davidson. If you want to get her steamed, just walk by the collator and yell, "Triumph rules!" or "Them Suzukis are pretty good machines!" She couldn't care less about poetry, especially the kind they put in this magazine.

But when I wheeled over with the skid that day, she started glancing at Naomi's poetry while she was feeding it into the collator.

"Hey, this ain't bad," she said. "This is the first time I've seen anything in here worth two shakes. Listen to this one. It's about karma. I love poems about karma."

"You don't have to read the poem, Charvyn, because I know it by heart already," I said, and recited a line from memory.

Charvyn just stared at me with her mouth open and said, "Go on, say some more. That's pretty. Did you write that?"

"My girlfriend, Naomi Thigpen, did," I told her, puffing up.

"Go on," she said. "Can I have your autograph?"

"Why do you want my autograph?"

"Because you know her and she's in a national magazine. You think you could get her to write a Harley poem?"

"I'll try," I said, and gave Charvyn my autograph. She took it and folded it twice and stuck it in her purse.

"I hope they print more of her poems," she said. "Usually, I can't make baby sense out of their poems. It's like they just want to sound big, show how much they know. And you know what else? The print's too small and fancy. If they don't want nobody to read their magazine, why don't they just come right out and stop printing?"

Charvyn told me this like I was one of the magazine's editors

all of a sudden, like I had something to do with the way the magazine was run. Then I thought about it, and I figured for this one
issue, I was an editor. A guest editor.

The little chicken-headed man on my lawn must be one of the
real editors. I figure as long as he's made the trip all the way from
New York, I might as well teach him a few things about what people
want to read.

"You want to hear good poetry?" I say.

"Yes!" he screams. He's still on his knees. Now he reaches his
arms over his head, his face lifted to the rising sun.

"Wait a second," I say, and go to the nightstand and pick up
the same issue of the magazine he's holding.

"Lawton," Naomi says when I return. "I want some straight
answers from you."

"I'm nothing but straight," I say. "We'll talk as soon as I get
rid of this lunatic."

"He's no lunatic," Naomi says, gesturing to the man, who still
has his arms raised, his face lifted like he's ready for the Second
Coming. He hasn't moved an inch. "He's suffering some deep
wound, some horrible sorrow," Naomi says. "If you were sensitive,
you'd see that."

"I'm sensitive," I say. "I love you. I love your poetry. Didn't I
send them off for you? Isn't that sensitive enough? Was Roger that
sensitive? Did he show you that much faith?"

Naomi doesn't have an answer for that, but she looks confused.
"Here!" I yell down to the man. "Here is some damn fine poetry."
And I start to read another of Naomi's poems.

Mother Nature's Abortion

Wood nymphs and sprites are dying of pollution
So are unicorns and fairies
Oh, what is the solution?

Smokestacks belch their foul fumes
While Puck and Bacchus gag
The leprechauns and elves are doomed!

Once-mighty Zeus drinks acid rain.
Hobbits hobble around on crutches.
Even happy Buddha cannot hide his pain.

Mother Nature has had an abortion
No one even tried to stop
This ecological disaster of immense proportions.

I look up from the page and see the man is holding his own copy of the magazine and has been following the words as I read them. He pauses for a moment, his lips still moving on the word *proportions*. Then he looks up at me, his eyes shining. He seems as moved as I am. He throws back his head and howls like a coyote. "Whoop whoop whoop whoop WOOOOO!"

Naomi looks dazed. She touches her head with her fingertips and says, "I don't feel so well. I think I'll lie down for a bit."

"Naomi," I say, and put my hand on her shoulder, but she trails away without a word and lies down on the bed, her face blank, her eyes open, staring at the ceiling. She looks dead.

I want to kill this man on my lawn, but I know I can't. I know that Naomi would leave me forever if I touched him.

"I'm waiting," he yells to me in a singsong.

"For what?"

"The poetry you promised."

I look back at the bed. Naomi has one of my pillows over her face.

"Now look what you've done," I tell the man.

"What *I've* done," he says, standing up slowly, a silly grin on his face, "is nothing compared to what you've done." He tears out a page from the magazine. He rips off a corner and starts to eat it. "From now on," he says, "I will dedicate my life to eating every issue of this magazine. With a circulation of two hundred thousand, do you know how long that will take me? It's nearly an impossible task. I will have to enlist the support of my friends, my lover, my mother, for *God's sake*. My mother will eat Naomi Thigpen's poems for breakfast, lunch, and dinner."

The man collapses on the ground, flat on his back. Then he swings his legs into the air and supports his backside with his hands. He starts making bicycle-pedaling motions with his legs. "Faster, faster!" he yells at the sky.

Someone touches me on the arm. I turn around and see Naomi. Her hair is unwashed and frizzy. She still has that paleness to her skin. It's so white and thin, it looks like it might tear if she smiles. She's not smiling now. She never smiles. I try to touch her cheek, but she pulls back.

"I'm dressed, Lawton," she says, and walks out of the room. I hear her feet on the steps. The door slams and she's out on the front walk, heading quickly for her car, past the man with his legs in the air, pedaling an invisible bicycle.

Long after she's gone, the man keeps doing that, and I wonder why. If things don't make sense, then where are we? You can't just bicycle-pedal on someone's lawn and expect him to stand for it. I turn away and go to the bedroom wall. I look at the place where I punched my fist through the plaster. All that feeling's gone now. I could never do something like that again. To tell the truth, I'm afraid to go downstairs and face that guy.

I lie down in bed and smell that bayberry scent that always reminds me of Naomi. I reach out to the nightstand and touch Naomi's crystals, which she's forgotten. I put them over my heart and say the Pledge of Allegiance. I whisper it. It always brings tears to my eyes.

Outside, I can almost hear the whirring of the pedals cutting the morning into smaller and smaller slices.

SLEEPING OVER

THE SECOND-TO-LAST KID ON THE BUS was a boy named
Randy Yam. Randy had red hair and freckles and seemed to wear
the same clothes to school every day. His mother had once been
our cleaning lady for a couple of months. She was fat and was missing some teeth, and had the most powerful smell of anyone I'd
ever met. My mother said she ate clay, and I figured maybe that's
why she smelled so bad. When she came over to clean once a week,
I had to leave the house, and even if I came home hours later, the
smell would still be there, and I had to breathe through my mouth
the rest of the day. Her son, Randy, didn't have an odor, but he
might as well have because you couldn't get near him. If you so
much as looked in his direction, he'd say you were staring at him, call
you a fag, and the next day he'd be waiting for you after school. It

hadn't happened to me, but it had happened to Fred Mink and Steve Wanger and George Trover and Roger Dansom. He just hated people staring at him. And what was *looking* to others was staring to him.

I stayed away, curled up on the cracked vinyl bus seat, growing sick to my stomach on bus fumes. I kept my back to Randy, so there was no way I could be accused of staring at him. But when he got off the bus, I always watched where he went. He headed through an immense field with overgrown weeds and a few scraggly trees. There wasn't a house in sight. Just this wide plain and hills off in the distance. If he lived in the hills, you'd think they could have found a road closer to home to let him off at. Maybe he and his mom slept out in the open and ate the dirt underneath them like my mom said. As the bus pulled off, I headed to the back and watched as he plunged through the weeds, but I never saw where it was he lived.

I wanted to become his best friend.

I was the last kid let off the bus, not because I lived that far out in Athens County, but because the bus route made a long loop like a shepherd's crook and my house was at the end of the crook. When we first moved in, the neighborhood hadn't been a neighborhood at all, just hills and a couple of farms and a large gully created from a dried-out lake. Our two-story aluminum-sided house sat at first at the top of the small valley, but before my parents bought it, the house slid down the hill in a thunderstorm. The developers just rebuilt it where it landed, and that's when we moved in. We were the only people around for a mile, and the place was surrounded by trees. In the mornings, guinea hens from a nearby farm would cluster in our yard and I'd chase them in circles. Then the developers started putting up cardboard houses in all the fields, a day or two apart, until there were twenty-five houses scrunched together. First the foundation was laid, then the workers put up a black cardboard skeleton, and then they put up the siding.

Families moved into about half the houses, one after another, but then they stopped, and the rest of the houses stood empty. In front of our house, there was a small road that led nowhere. It just trickled off into the dirt of a hill. There were almost a dozen unoccupied houses on this road.

Sometimes, I dreamed about them. I was walking down the road past all the houses, and each one had a single candle burning in the window. A mist started to appear in front of me and I knew I should go inside a house, but I was afraid I'd be trapped there. So I kept walking down the road until I came to another empty house, but I realized it shouldn't have been empty because it was ours.

One afternoon on the bus, we had nearly reached his field. I had my back to him as usual, but I felt like he was watching me, and I didn't know why. I turned around and looked at a poster warning kids not to accept rides from strangers. It showed a man in a Dracula cape holding out an ice-cream cone to a girl in pigtails.

"You want to sleep over at my house?" I said, like I was saying it to no one in particular.

"Sure," said the bus driver, a skinny old man who looked like LBJ. "But I'll have to check home with my wife first." He looked at me in the wide rearview mirror.

I thought he was serious, and didn't know what my mom would think if I brought the bus driver home with me. One time, I'd invited my teacher for dinner because I had a crush on her. She said she'd be delighted, and asked me what time to show up.

"Nine," I said. Nine was actually my bedtime. I suppose I imagined my mother saying, "Well, we've already eaten, but this is David's bedtime. So if you want to sleep over, you can."

When I arrived home that evening, I forgot all about my teacher. She showed up at nine sharp and rang the doorbell.

"David, go see who that is," said my mother.

"No," I said.

"Come on," she said. "Go see who it is. Tell them I'll be down in a minute."

I went downstairs, looked through the window, and saw my teacher dressed up with a fur collar and her hair made up. She saw me and waved. I waved back and ran upstairs.

"Who is it?" my mother asked.

"Nobody."

My mother shook her head and walked downstairs to see for herself. I tagged behind her saying, "She wants to eat. Don't let her in."

"What's your mom fixin' us for supper?" the driver asked me.

I looked at him in horror. He couldn't come over, but I didn't have the heart to tell him. "Lima beans," I said.

"Mmm, I *love* lima beans!" the driver said.

We were coming to the bend in the road where Randy was let off. The bus stopped. It was too late. I wondered if the bus driver would like any of my toys, if he'd even fit in my bed. Randy stood up to leave.

"Oh, you know what?" the driver said. "I just remembered. I got to give my pet boa constrictor a flea dip tonight. Maybe I can sleep over next week. Why don't you see if Randy there can take my place?"

Relieved, I ran back to Randy, looked him straight in the eye, and asked, did he want to sleep over?

"You like Creepy Crawlers?" I asked Randy as we walked down the road with the empty houses. I didn't know what he liked, and it was important to know. If he liked what I liked, then we could be friends.

"Yeah," he said.

"You like Incredible Edibles?" I asked.

"Yeah," he said. He had his hands jammed in his corduroy windbreaker.

"Me, too," I said, though I really hated them. They always tasted burnt and like plastic after you cooked them in their molds.

"*Dark Shadows?*" I asked.

"What?"

"Barnabas," I said, and exposed my incisors and stretched my hands into monster hands.

He looked blankly at me.

"*Laugh-In?*"

He nodded.

"I carry the torch, ooh-ooh," I sang from a skit on the Olympics. It was the most hilarious thing when Goldie Hawn sang that, but Randy was looking at me like I was crazy.

"Don't you watch *Laugh-In?*" I asked.

"No," he said. "I don't watch much TV. But we got one. It's a color TV."

"You have a color TV?" I asked. And he didn't like to watch it? None of my friends had a color TV except for Gil Greer, the son of the bank president.

I didn't call Randy a liar. I wanted to live. I admitted we didn't have color. We'd had our TV since I was born. It looked like *Sputnik,* which was launched that same year. "Can I come over and see it sometime?" I asked.

"No," he said.

"None of these houses has anyone living in them," I said, pointing to the split-levels on either side of us.

"Why not?" Randy asked. "Something wrong with them? They haunted?"

"You believe in ghosts?" I asked.

"I seen a ghost," he said. "My daddy. Before he died, he come visit us all the time. He'd sleep in my bed with me. Used to keep a bottle in my dresser. One night, he come into the room and just stared down at me, didn't say nothin', didn't crawl into bed with me or nothin'. That's when I knew he was dead. He come and stared at me every night for three months."

"Is that the truth? Were you scared?" I asked.

Randy didn't say anything. He picked up a rock and threw it toward the house closest to us. The rock hit the aluminum siding and made a pinging sound. Randy started walking across the lawn, which wasn't a lawn at all, but trampled straw and mud.

"Where you going?" I yelled. "That's private property."

I'd never even thought about going inside one of the houses. Ever since my nightmares, I was a little scared of them. But Randy was fearless and I followed. After all, he'd slept with a ghost for three months. The door wasn't locked and we went inside. The house was completely empty except for a tan carpet that sponged down when you walked through it. The walls were spotless. There was no furniture. Randy went ahead of me, opening all the doors and flicking the switches even though none of them worked. In the bathroom, there wasn't even a toilet, just some pipes.

Randy started unbuckling his belt.

"What you doing?"

"Taking a dump."

"We have a real bathroom at my house," I said. Randy didn't pay any attention to me. He slipped his pants to his ankles, then his underpants.

"What you looking at?" he said.

"Nothing," I said, and turned away.

"Randy?" I said.

"What?"

"Why does your mom smell so bad?" I said. I'd been dying to

ask him. My mom didn't use her as a cleaning lady anymore because of the woman's smell. I figured he'd tell me since he'd already told me about seeing a ghost.

But as soon as the words escaped me, I knew I'd done a stupid thing. Talking about someone's mother, even though I didn't mean anything by it. She smelled bad and that was a fact. But Randy would beat you up for anything. Randy had beaten up Tommy Turnbull for calling him a son of a gun. And Tommy hadn't meant anything by it. Tommy just liked the phrase and had been saying it for a week. He'd even come up to me and said it, punching me in the arm. "How's it hanging, you old son of a gun?" he said, and laughed. Tommy Turnbull was infested with cooties, so no one minded too much when Randy took him out.

I heard Randy buckling his belt so I turned around. He looked thoughtful for a second, like he was trying to think of an answer. Then he said, "I'm going to kick your butt."

Randy approached me now, one hand in a fist, the other pulling his belt tight.

"Wait!" I screamed. "Don't do that."

"Why not?"

"I was just testing you."

"You was?"

I hadn't thought about what I was going to say, but words tumbled out of me. "You're very insecure. You don't have to be everyone's friend. You don't have to buy everyone's friendship." This is what my dad had said to my mom after the most recent party she threw. My mother was always throwing cocktail parties and my dad said we couldn't afford them.

"What do you mean, insecure?"

"Stop trying to be everyone's friend," I repeated, a little more uncertainly.

"I ain't," he said.

"Good," I said. "You see? Don't you feel better?" This is another thing that my dad always said to my mom after he gave her a lecture.

Randy looked at me with a dazed expression, but he still didn't seem convinced. "Why'd you say that about my mama? She don't smell. You better say you're sorry." Randy looked like he was about to cry.

I said I was sorry, thinking I was out of danger, but that seemed to make Randy angrier. He wanted to know one good reason he shouldn't kick my butt. I told him about Gandhi. He was one of my mom's friends or something. I'd probably met him at one of her cocktail parties. All I remembered was the phrase *passive distance*, and that's what I told Randy about. I said that when someone had told Gandhi that his mother smelled, he did passive distance instead of kicking his butt. Gandhi was a great man, I said, and great men thought alike. I babbled for about fifteen minutes. I wore Randy down, and after a while he smiled and didn't seem angry anymore. He seemed genuinely happy he hadn't beaten me up. He put his arm around my shoulder and we walked out of the empty house. Somehow, I'd survived.

Randy stayed for dinner but hardly touched his food. My mom made ratatouille that night. She was always making things like that, so I was used to it. But Randy wasn't. He asked if we had any burgers, and just sat there and stared at his plate full of vegetables.

After dinner, we watched *Wild, Wild West*, and pretended we had magic powers and could make James T. West and Artemus Gordon say and do stupid things.

In the middle of the program, Chet Huntley came on and made a special announcement. I ran up with Randy to my mother's bedroom and told her.

"Mom, some doctor's been shot." At first, I'd thought it was Dr. Goldsmith, one of my mom and dad's friends who always came to her cocktail parties.

"What? Who was it?" she said, sitting up in bed.

"Dr. King. It was on TV."

"Oh God," my mother said, and sank back down.

My mother explained. He was a great man who wanted black and white people to live together in peace, and the rich and the poor to work together for a better world. That sounded like someone my mother would like.

"He was some nigger?" Randy asked.

My mother sat up in bed. "Take your friend downstairs, David," she said, glaring at me like I'd said the forbidden word. "Maybe it would be best for him to spend the night at his own house."

Despite my mother's disapproval, Randy and I became best friends after that night. I had other best friends, but Randy was my newest. No one else could get close to him, so I was *his only* best friend.

That week, staring contests became the big thing at school. We each bet a dime. I was terrible. I wanted to win, but I kept blinking. Randy refused to play, said he thought it was stupid. But I had a feeling about him. Something made me think that Randy would rather die than blink. I cornered him in the bathroom and said I wanted to be his manager.

"What's that?" he asked.

"It means if you win, I take 50 percent of the net and 100 percent of the gross."

"What's the gross?"

"I don't know," I admitted.

"I don't like no one staring at me," he said.

"This is different," I said. "Business is business."

And so Randy started learning how to stare. I had been right about him. He was unstoppable. But to make sure he could last without blinking, I'd take him to the bathroom before a match and squeeze a little water from an eyedropper into each of his eyes. All that week, we raked in the cash. Many of the other starers had grudges against Randy: Tommy Turnbull, Roger Dansom, Thad Keller, George Trover. The only starer Randy didn't topple was Steve Wanger. We didn't call him Steve. Sometimes, we called him Wanger, Wang-doodle, or the Hang Wang. Steve made explosions during class. During a math drill or a geography lesson, we'd suddenly hear this long drawn-out whistle and then Steve would go, "*Kerplow!*" So we called him Boomer. Everyone had a nickname. Mine was Sherlock, since my last name was Watson. Or sometimes I was called Fartson or Notson. The only person in school who didn't have a nickname was Randy Yam, even though we could have done incredible things with his name. Kids just called him Randy.

Boomer and Randy had started on Friday afternoon to stare at each other in the hall, where most of our contests were held. Boomer's strategy was simple: lock his gaze on Randy and try to distract him with explosions. You would have thought you were at Fort Sumter the way Steve carried on. A crowd was gathered around them. I was bent close to Randy, staring at him staring at Steve. I saw the corners of Randy's eyes tremble and I knew he was going to blink.

"Boom! Boom!" Steve yelled, making a mushroom cloud with his hands. I'd never seen him make such a large explosion. Spittle bubbled from the corners of his mouth. He was going for broke.

Lately, Steve had been expanding his repertoire to include imitations of police-band radios. "Squawk, scrunch," Steve said, staring hard at Randy. "This is Adam-12. Do you read? Yes, we have the suspect in custody, a black male Caucasian."

"Bell's going to ring," I shouted, and stepped in between them.

The other kids groaned and someone shouted, "What'd you do that for, Fartson?"

Luckily, the bell did go off and I explained that I just wanted everything to be fair, that we should postpone the contest until next week. I also thought it was unfair for Boomer to keep making explosions and police-radio sounds, but no one agreed with me. Even Randy seemed to take Steve's explosions well. "It don't bother me none," he said.

Still, I was afraid that Randy was going to lose a rematch. "We need to practice technique," I told him. "Let's go to your house."

We didn't need to go to his house to practice, but I wanted to see where he lived and I also wanted to watch his color TV.

"No," Randy said.

We took the bus home and sat together. Randy didn't say a word the whole way home. He looked out the window the entire ride, and when I asked him if he thought he could beat Steve Wanger next week, he said, "I don't know. I don't care." When the driver stopped at Randy's field, Randy stood up and walked down the aisle without saying good-bye. Suddenly, he turned around and said, "I changed my mind. You can come over tonight if you want." He smiled when he said this, but he looked strange, almost like he was afraid I'd say no. I figured he just wasn't used to inviting kids over. I didn't know anyone who'd been to his house.

"Sure," I said.

The driver looked disappointed.

"What about me?" he said. "I thought it was my turn to sleep over."

The bus stayed in the road after we were let off, and I heard the driver laughing and calling faintly, "Tell me when it's my turn, boys." Then I heard the gears start, the doors close, and the bus crunching down the gravel road.

We walked about a hundred yards into the field, to an opening in the ground like someone's cellar—two wooden doors with chipped paint the dark green color of picnic tables in a state park. The doors were in the middle of a concrete slab about the size and shape of half a basketball court. Off to the side was a rusted Lark, half-hidden in the weeds behind a leafless tree.

"Wow," I said, really impressed. "You live underground?"

I hadn't known that Randy was that lucky. It was like living in the Batcave. No wonder he never wanted kids to see where he lived, any more than Bruce Wayne wanted visitors to see where *he* lived. They'd never want to leave.

"I brought David home with me!" Randy yelled from the top of the stairs.

I heard a faucet turn off. Mrs. Yam appeared below us, wiping her hands on her dress. Her arms were crossed, her head tilted like she had a question she wanted to ask.

"I see that," she said, and brushed some hair from her eyes. She scratched her arm and blew a quick breath, then glanced away. "I'm not fixin' anything special. Don't he want to come back some other night when I can fix something special for him?"

"David don't want nothin' special, do you, David?"

I shook my head. As long as it wasn't dirt or clay, I didn't care what she fixed. But she seemed unconvinced. She obviously didn't want me coming into her home. Maybe she was angry at my mom for not giving her any more housecleaning work.

"Either way," Randy said, "you gonna have to give him a ride home. Or else he'll have to walk. The bus left already."

Mrs. Yam set her chin to one side and then set it to the other side. She glanced behind her again, then back at Randy. She scratched an ear. "Guess you're right," she said. "Guess I'll have to give him a ride home no matter what. Come on down, boys. I'll see what I can whip up."

Down in Randy's house, which was one big room, it felt damp and smelled like clay. The floor was uneven, covered with linoleum, but the packed clay underneath showed through all the cracks. In the middle of the floor was a drain. There was hardly any furniture: a couple of cots and a bed shoved up against the wall, a dresser, a pine chest. Near the middle of the room stood a sink and a wood stove with a pipe leading into the ceiling. At the far corner of the room, a man sat in a rocking chair staring at a color TV.

I was amazed. I was drawn to the TV like it was the vision of some angel. How could Randy be so lucky? Not only did he live in the Batcave, but he had a color TV, too. I approached the TV slowly. The man watching the television was staring at me. I'd never been stared at like that before and it made me feel strange.

"Who's that?" he said.

"Just one of Randy's little friends," said Mrs. Yam.

"Well, bring him over here," the man said. "Watch some TV with me." The man had silver slicked-back hair, wide blue eyes, and a long chin. I couldn't tell how old he was. Both he and Mrs. Yam looked as old as my grandparents, but I'd heard my mother tell my father once that Mrs. Yam was ten years younger than she was.

"Yeah, let's watch TV," I said.

"No," said Randy.

"Come on, let's watch TV."

"I said no."

"Go on now, join your daddy," Mrs. Yam said. His daddy? I'd thought his daddy was dead, and had come visiting from the other side. That's what he'd told me at the empty house. He'd also told me he had a color TV. I hadn't believed him then, but it had turned out true. Maybe he hadn't been lying about his daddy either.

I brushed the chair Randy's father sat in. I wondered, if he touched me, would I feel it? Would his body pass through mine?

We sat on the cold floor beside the man. "Ask your friend what he wants to see," the man said to Randy. That shocked me. No one's dad had ever asked me what I wanted to see when I was at his house. Moms had asked me but never dads. You watched whatever he was watching, my dad included.

"I don't care," I said quietly. "This is good."

Let's Make a Deal was on. Someone had chosen the wrong

door. There was just a sheep behind it. For the first time, I saw the lovely Carol Merrill in color. I should have been thrilled, but all I could think of was Randy's father. The man just stared at me with a faint smile.

A commercial came on for Hawaiian Punch. The little man in the sun hat asked for a Hawaiian Punch and got laid out flat. He never learned, just like the rabbit who didn't know that Trix were for kids.

"Change the channel to *Death Valley Days*," the man told Randy.

"Randy tells me you-all been holding staring contests at school," the man said. "Is that the sort of thing you go in for?"

"I'm not very good," I admitted.

"Don't say that!" the man cried out. "You're just as good as you think you are. Think you can beat me?"

"No, sir."

"Sure you can," he said. "Let's try."

The man started staring at me. I looked at him and then I looked at Randy. I recognized something I'd never seen in him before. I couldn't imagine anything that would scare Randy.

"Look," Randy said, pointing a finger at the set like there was something special on it. But it was a commercial, just the Borax mule team marching through Death Valley.

"No fair," the man said. "Lookin' away's the same as cheatin'."

I stared at the old man and he stared back. I saw where Randy got his staring powers from. I also saw why he didn't like it much. I didn't want to stare at the man because he was an adult, but there didn't seem to be any way to make him stop.

His eyes dropped to my belt buckle. He still stared, but not at my eyes. He wasn't playing by the rules. And he'd mentioned them not a second before. I thought I'd won. But he didn't say anything. He just kept staring and I didn't know what to do except stare back at the top of his head.

"You want to see my war wound?" he asked, still staring at my buckle.

"No thanks," I said.

The man started rolling up his trousers. From the corner of my eye, I saw that his legs were waxy-looking, ridged and welted, and the colors ran from red to purple. He smiled as I looked at him, and said, "Go ahead, touch it."

Randy hit me in the nose. One second I was staring at his father, the next I was cupping my hands around my nose and groaning.

I knew Randy would hit me someday, but I thought I'd have to do or say something stupid first. I hadn't expected to be hit out of the blue.

I didn't expect Mr. Yam to laugh either, but he did. "You look like a peg-legged man at an ass-kicking. I guess I won." Then he turned to Randy and said, "I didn't need your help." Randy shrugged.

Mrs. Yam rushed over to me and hovered there. She seemed to think I was dying. "Oh Lord," she said. "What a sight. Your mama's never goin' to forgive me. Come, let's get you cleaned up at least."

Mr. Yam tried to stand up. He teetered in a crouch, half out of his seat and half in. "I can take care of him," Mr. Yam said. "You just go fix supper."

"Supper can wait," Mrs. Yam said, taking me by an elbow and hurrying me over to the sink like I might bleed to death. The worry in her voice scared me. I wondered how bad I looked.

Mr. Yam followed us to the sink and took me by the arm. "I'm hungry," he said. "I'll clean him up." I didn't know what to think about this family. First their son socked me in the nose for no good reason, then his parents started arguing over who was going to clean me up.

Mr. Yam turned to Randy, who was watching him. "What you lookin' at?"

"Nothin'."

"Yeah, and I'm Marie of Romania," Randy's dad said. I wondered who Marie of Romania was and why he thought he was her.

Randy didn't say anything, but stared at his father intensely, the way he'd looked at me that time I'd mentioned his mama's smell. I noticed something then. I didn't smell her. Maybe Randy had knocked something loose in my nose.

"I think I better be going home," I said, holding onto my nose.

"Why'd you hit him, Randy?" Mr. Yam asked, but he didn't seem angry as much as disappointed.

"Because," Randy said.

"That's not a very good reason. You gonna say you're sorry?"

"I guess."

"Say it then."

Randy must have apologized to me, but I didn't hear him because I had a strange feeling on my neck, and it made me turn around. Randy's dad wasn't smiling anymore, but staring at me.

"You stayin' for supper?" Mr. Yam asked me. "You sleepin' over?" First the bus driver and now Randy's dad. You'd think adults would want to sleep over with people their own size.

"I've got to get home," I said. After the way they'd treated me, I was sure they'd fix me dirt on a platter for supper.

Mr. Yam fiddled with one of the buttons on his shirt.

"No wonder none of your friends come callin' with you beatin' on them all the time," he told Randy. "I swear. You can't just go through life shittin' and fallin' backwards. If you gonna act like a wild dog, maybe you'd like to sleep out in the car."

"Yes, sir."

"And give him your shirt." Randy did like he was told, and stood there bare-chested beside us. He clasped his arms around himself and shivered. Then he headed up the stairs. Mr. Yam went back to his TV set, lost in *Death Valley Days*.

Mrs. Yam scrubbed me down in a hurry, like she had her mind on other things. I might as well have been a potato the way she scrubbed me. The sink had a deep basin and was made of steel, and the cold water drummed into it as Mrs. Yam washed my face and neck.

"I guess I *better* take you on home," Mrs. Yam said. "Your mama's not going to like the sight of you."

Randy's dad gave me one last look. He seemed like he was going to say something, but then he looked at Mrs. Yam, who stared back at him. They seemed to be having their own staring contest. Then Mrs. Yam lowered her eyes.

"We won't be gone long," she said.

"Don't you take Randy with you!" Mr. Yam yelled after us. "I want to have a word with him."

No one seemed to care that Randy was standing outside without his shirt. I sat in the front seat with Mrs. Yam, and Randy climbed into the back. "Your dad says you can't come along," I told him. I was pretty angry with him, hitting me for no good reason. But Mrs. Yam didn't tell him to get out of the car. Instead, she gunned the motor. There was a suitcase that looked like it was covered with burlap sitting back with Randy. He popped it open and pulled out a T-shirt. I wondered if he slept out in the car often, if his mom kept a stockpile for him. He slipped on the shirt and leaned forward in his seat. His mother looked straight ahead.

"Hurry, Mom," he said.

When we arrived at my house, I saw that all the lights were on and there were people milling around. It was one of my mother's cocktail parties. I made out well at these parties. My mother let me have sips of her drinks, and vodka-soaked olives and maraschino cherries. And she always made onion-cheese pie for the guests, and that was my favorite. But for some reason, I didn't want to go inside that night.

"I think if we practice, we can beat Steve Wanger," I said, turning around in the seat. Randy looked at me like he didn't recognize who I was and had no idea what I was talking about. He looked so much older than me. That must be why he was so hard to get to know, I thought. That was why he didn't like the same toys, didn't watch TV. He was too much older. He was like the teacher I had a crush on, the bus driver, the people at my mother's cocktail party. He knew things I didn't know. To ask him to sleep over was as dumb as asking the bus driver.

"Randy, say good-bye to your friend. We're leavin'."

"Sorry I busted you in the nose," Randy told me. "I meant to sock you, but I didn't want to. Go on, hit me back. Gimme a Hawaiian Punch."

A Hawaiian Punch? Only the little man in the sun hat on TV ever said that, and he said it over and over again. Everyone else knew better. If you asked for a Hawaiian Punch, you were fair game. Randy really looked like he wanted me to hit him, like he'd be happy if I did. But I didn't want to. The thought of it made me feel queasy.

"That's all right," I said, though I wasn't sure what made it all right. I'd expected worse. I don't know. Maybe my nose broken or bit off. Maybe death. I'd thought it would hurt like the dentist, something sharp and splitting. But this was a wider pain that began in my nose like a head cold and spread out around the bones of my cheeks. Was that all it was? My nose was still bloody and I licked my lip where the blood ran. A punch in the nose. This wasn't so bad. I could survive this.

I knew I wouldn't see Randy again. I'm not sure how, but I knew. Maybe the suitcase in the car or his mother's urgent tone. Or even Randy's apology to me. Randy wasn't the kind who apologized.

After they left, I went inside and made my way through the crowd to my mother. I walked among them and hardly looked up at their faces.

"What happened to you?" my mother said when she saw me.

"Nothing," I said.

"Look at you," she said. "Don't tell me nothing happened. Was it that Randy Yam? I don't want you seeing him anymore."

"I won't," I said. I didn't know why Randy and his mom were running away, but I hoped they weren't like me. Every time I ran away, I was home that night for supper.

"And what's that smell?" she asked.

I didn't have to answer because my mother's attention was distracted by Dr. Goldsmith, who came by and said, "Sylvia, one of these days I'm going to kidnap you and take you to a desert isle, where we'll live on canapés and caviar."

"We'll need to wash it down with something," she said, laughing.

Seeing my chance, I escaped to my room. I felt tired and went to sleep almost immediately. But in the middle of the night, I awoke and went to my window. Outside, in one of the empty model houses, I thought I saw a light in one of the windows. I wasn't afraid. It wasn't like one of my nightmares. It wasn't a ghost. I stared at the window until my eyes hurt.

AN INTRUDER

THE QUEEN'S FIRST THOUGHT UPON AWAKENING is, Oh my, not again, and this one's coal black. Her thoughts are not for her own safety. They never are. Her thoughts always settle on the larger ramifications. Like the crows in front of the palace, the queen's thoughts are ponderous and never take flight. They pace mutely and passively in front of their station.

"I didn't mean to wake you," the man says from the foot of the bed.

The man at the foot of her bed has his hair in that extravagant West Indian style. The prince consort said once he quite liked that fashion, and might consider trying it out himself if not for the paucity of his hair, but he'd been smashed when he said that.

The man looks nearly fifty, a slender fellow with a beaked nose and a long drawn face. "Young man," she addresses him. Everyone is young to her. You cannot count her age in mortal years. "I am your queen and you are in my bedchamber."

The man stands and bumps his head on the canopy. "I mean no disrespect. I've come here for what belongs to me."

The queen nods her head as the man speaks each word. His speech is musical. Her hat tips off her head and she straightens it. This is how she always sleeps, fully clothed in a modest dress, her purse by her side, a plain hat on her head. She keeps her body straight when she sleeps. She didn't always sleep this way, but before she did, she frequently had nightmares. Sometimes, she'd be walking past the crows in front of the palace dressed only in a white nightgown, jeered by thousands. Other times, she simply saw herself growing. Or she imagined herself a coin, the face worn thin by the hands and pockets of her people. She enjoys dreams as little as she enjoys free-flying thought. Now that she sleeps like the queen, fully clothed, her dreams no longer bother her.

"It's entirely possible you're looking for something that's rightfully yours," she says. Best not to alarm him. "But I doubt anything here belongs to you, except in the most general sense. I assume you're a subject of the realm?"

"Yes, Mom, more citizen than you can reckon. I'm your own son, your flesh and blood."

There's not the slightest chance, the most remote possibility that what this man says is true . . . Well, yes, maybe a slight chance. The gardener, of course. Long before she was queen.

"I just want what's rightfully mine, a mother's love."

She stares at him.

"That's quite impossible," she says.

"I could ask for more, you know. I'm older than the crown prince by five years."

These Jamaicans! Next thing you know, her Paki son will want to be acknowledged. And maybe her son from New Jersey. And her daughter from The Gambia. Oh, she was a wild one when she was young, back when the press was more respectful and knew how to keep a secret.

"Are you married?" she asks, hoping to change the subject, but also out of true concern.

"Very happily, Mom," he says, smiling broadly at her. "To the most lovely woman in the world. And I have many children. You'd be proud of them. You can smell the royalty in them. You want to see their pictures?"

She surprises herself by sitting up in bed and saying, "Why yes, I think I do." After all, he is her son, and she's happy that at least one of her line has not botched his marriage. One by one, her son shows her the photos in his wallet. His wallet bulges with photos. She studies each picture closely, looking for the resemblances. She wishes she were young again. She wishes she'd set a better example.

Of course, acknowledgment is out of the question. It would only be an embarrassment and a burden for her, the nation, and even her Jamaican son and his family. Tonight, she will give him a mother's attention, a mother's ear, a mother's love. But in the morning, he will have to go. She will ring for the guards and they will take the man away. But what if they don't respond? Lately, they've become so undependable.

She lies back, just as her son is saying, "And this is little Betsy . . ."

She closes her eyes and says, "You were a mistake, weren't you? One of many. I should have known you'd find your way here sooner or later."

"All I'm asking for is what's rightfully mine," he says, "just a bit of your time, a little company." And then he prattles on with his photos. "And this is little Henry. And this is Ethelbert, my oldest, and Johnny. He's a troublemaker." How many children can one man have? "And this is little Mary. Mom! Mom! Don't you want to see young Richard, my favorite . . . ?"

SHINSAIBASHI

I RODE THE SUBWAY DOWN TO THE SHOPPING DISTRICT
called Shinsaibashi, and noticed a red-haired woman standing in
front of a department store. Giant red-and-white banners flapped
above her. The banners, written in bold kanji, looked severe and
militaristic, but I'm sure they simply exhorted shoppers to come
inside. For a moment, I forgot about my rendezvous with Chizuko.
I ran up to the woman and tapped her on the shoulder. "*Gaijin
desuka?*" I said. Rude, I know, but ten times a day someone came
up to me and asked *me* if I was a foreigner. The next question was
whether or not I'd help them practice English. Everyone wanted to
practice English. Not me, unless it was with another *gaijin*.

The red-haired woman turned around. I jumped back. I might
have screamed. Chizuko laughed, threw back her head, flaunted her
red hair in imitation of someone on a shampoo commercial.

"Surprise," she said, running out ahead of me. She turned around as though caught by a tether. "Don't I look stunning? Ravishing?" She pronounced *ravish* like *radish*.

She *looked* like a radish. I stood still. I've never been good at hiding my feelings. People say my eyes tell it all. And in Osaka, that sometimes got me into trouble. Once, when I visited one of my pupil's homes, I openly admired a hundred-year-old kimono in a display case. By the time I realized what I had said, it was too late. I might as well have asked them to gift-wrap it for me. After that, they wouldn't let me out of the house alive without the kimono. Another time, a student garbled an English phrase so badly that I had to hide my mouth in my fist to keep from laughing. This student was vice president of sales for the Samuda Trading Company, my employer. He was also Chizuko's father.

Everyone knew the meaning of my fist in my mouth. All his classmates. All his employees. His daughter, too. After that, Chizuko dropped my class. This was the first time I'd seen her since that day.

I scratched my ear and smiled at her. "You look . . . almost American," I said. "So where shall we go? Would you like to catch a movie?" I said this in a formal way, like some textbook practitioner of English.

Chizuko looked at her feet. Obviously, she knew how hideous I thought she'd made herself. I might as well have called her Bozo. But I preferred the traditional. My favorite time in Japan was around New Year's, when everyone wore bright new kimonos and strolled under parasols. That seemed natural. Red- or blonde-dyed hair seemed garish in contrast. Why pretend to be something you're not? I wondered. Still, I wished at that moment I knew something about pretense. That, after all, seemed to me the basic difference between me and the Japanese. Pretending you like something when you don't, or vice versa, or remaining impassive. Was that always wrong?

I don't know what I'd been thinking in the first place. I must have been crazy calling Chizuko and asking if she'd like to meet me for a date. "Yes, certainly!" Her voice had almost trembled. And now she'd shown up with red hair.

We walked politely down Shinsaibashi toward a theater. Shinsaibashi is long and narrow, and stretches for a couple of miles, sometimes enclosed, sometimes open to the sky. The old and the new mix here: a department store, a French bakery, a tea shop, a coffeehouse called the New York Cafe, a print shop, a video arcade, a pachinko parlor. Hundreds of black-haired shoppers hurried past us, many with shopping bags with slogans printed in English. Half of the slogans made no sense. One bag read, "REMEMBER! This bag is fashions. Both illustration and fresh-of-feeling. Born in the young power." Emblazoned on another were the words, "Hey Dude! Shock that retrograde and bust it."

We made polite conversation. We talked about her father. We talked about the growth over the last twenty years of the Samuda Trading Company. We didn't mention anything divisive. Whales or trade imbalances. Day-Glo red hair.

Finally, we came to a river with a wide footbridge. Several beggars rested along the railings. These scruffy men with hands outstretched looked forlorn and forgotten. No one paid them any attention. On the other bank, a giant mechanical crab loomed above a shop, crossing and uncrossing its claws. A movie theater stood beside the seafood store. A disaster film out of Hollywood was playing.

The theater was packed, and before the movie began, they played a newsreel. I liked the fact that they still played newsreels, even though this was more American than Japanese. But American theaters haven't shown newsreels since the early sixties, before I can remember. So watching newsreels seemed like an authentic Japanese custom to me. But this one wasn't so wonderful. It showed the emperor laying a wreath in Hiroshima. I moved my seat backward and forward. Everyone was silent, their eyes straight ahead, except for me. I looked around the theater and wondered what they were thinking. In the dark, you couldn't tell I was a *gaijin*. You couldn't make out the color of anyone's hair. I looked over at Chizuko but saw nothing on her face.

Then the film began and I listened to it in English while everyone else looked toward the lower right-hand corner, where the subtitles streamed down the screen.

Sometimes, I forgot what was going on, and just sat there tensely. I still felt disappointed. I liked traditional Japan. That's what I'd come here for. I'd often walk down an alley at night near where I lived, and I'd try to imagine myself in that same spot fifty years earlier. Obviously, things would have been much different. I imagined people spitting in my path. I imagined being marched at the point of a bayonet, jeered at, reviled. Of course, I didn't want that, but at the same time, I did. Or maybe I wanted to be one of the people on the other side, spitting at the captured American.

This is what I was thinking during the movie, and so I missed most of it. When the lights came up, Chizuko looked brightly at me and said, "That was something really good I think!"

I nodded and smiled. But inside, I felt so foolish. Misleading her. Misleading myself. Anything I'd felt toward her in class had disappeared. Another problem was the age difference. She was barely out of high school.

She told me I didn't need to accompany her home, but I insisted, and on the subway ride she sat between me and a man who looked as old and scruffy as one of the beggars on the bridge. He poked her in the shoulder and pointed to me. He said something I couldn't catch, and then she said something, and he made what sounded like a speech, with elaborate arm gestures. He kept looking over at me and mugging, making his eyes wide. I didn't understand what he said, but he seemed awfully rude.

Chizuko put her hand over her mouth. She looked like she was stifling a laugh.

"What did he say?" I said.

"He asked if you were American," she said in a serious tone. "He said he wished all Americans were as skinny as you because then we would have won the war."

Oh well, that didn't bother me. "Tell him I wish there'd been no reason for the war in the first place," I told Chizuko. "Tell him I'm sorry what's happened to Japanese culture since then."

I looked past her eyes to her hair, then back to her eyes.

Chizuko's whole face changed. Any hint of a smile disappeared. But she didn't look angry. The only thing that looked angry was her hair. She looked the way her father had looked when I bit my laughter into my fist. Not angry. Not hurt. But resigned. Something fatal and sad had seemed to cross his face, like a small shock wave passing through his heart. But he didn't want to alarm anyone. Instead, he smiled and nodded slightly and then said, "Excuse me, teacher. I'm very sorry." When he said that, I felt a tremor pass through my heart, too. My amusement seemed so callous and hollow. I went on with the lesson. I didn't make a big deal of it. At least I knew to do that much.

And maybe I should have apologized now. To Chizuko. Or the old man who thought I was skinny. I needed to apologize to someone.

Chizuko turned to the old man and said something, but not what I'd said. My rudimentary knowledge of Japanese told me that much. He nodded like she'd said something very wise.

I took the train back to Shinsaibashi after seeing Chizuko home. I passed by the same bridge. The beggars still sat there. Beyond, the mechanical crab still waved. I bought some bean curd jelly from a woman with a handcart, and ate the jelly as I walked along. The shops were closing up now, the people thinning out. I finished my bean curd in front of a pachinko parlor where bells clanged and cigarette smoke hovered. I licked my fingers and walked on.

Then I came to a tea store still open. From the window, I saw an old woman in a kimono sitting at the counter. The center of the store was empty, but the walls were lined with canisters of loose green tea.

I felt vaguely guilty, and thought maybe I should buy Chizuko a canister of tea. I didn't want her to remember me as an impolite American, a savage. I could imagine her home now with her father, both of them silently sharing the humiliation they'd suffered at my hands. Why couldn't I learn the subtleties of Japanese social interaction? Why couldn't I make my eyes go blank and stop betraying me? Maybe I'd buy two canisters of tea. The best. Even though their best tasted terribly bitter to me.

When I walked inside, the old woman in her kimono bowed. She smiled and spoke rapidly, guiding me gently toward the front counter. She acted as if she'd never seen a *gaijin* before. I bowed back and smiled.

She moved her hands up and down, motioning me to sit. I sat and she smiled again and bowed. Then she disappeared into the back room.

I had a bad feeling about this. I figured that since this was a tea shop, she was probably going back there to fix me some tea. And since I was a foreigner, someone special, she'd almost definitely bring me the best grade of tea, the most expensive she could find.

A couple of minutes later, she returned with a clay pot and a cup. She sat in front of me and poured a big cup of tea.

Then she handed it to me and nodded her head. I nodded back.

I'd been thinking about this cup of tea. I'd known it was coming and so I was able to prepare myself. No matter how bitter it tasted, I was determined I would not wince. I would not blink. I would not allow my cheeks to suck in or my eyes to bulge. My eyes would be mirrors, and all I would allow myself would be a smile, a nod of the head, and then I'd tell her how delicious it tasted.

I took the first sip, feeling like Socrates. In fact, this tea must have been a little like hemlock, because the effects were similar. It tasted so awful that my tongue went numb and my whole mouth felt woolly. After that, my throat constricted. I tried to swallow. The first sip was hard to keep down. But I forced it through. Then it hit my stomach and I felt two sharp pains on the right side of my abdomen.

The old woman leaned toward me eagerly, a broad smile on her face. In one more second, I was going to retch.

I thought pure thoughts. I imagined heaven. I saw myself helping this woman across a crowded street.

Then it was over. But that was only the first sip. I closed my eyes dreamily, as though I'd sipped ambrosia. Then I downed the rest in one steady gulp, and paused a second to see if it would stay put. I set the cup loudly on the counter and exclaimed, "*Oishee!*"

The woman smiled even more broadly and bowed. I'd won. I saw that she was fooled. She thought I loved it. I was so happy I hardly knew what was going on when she lifted the clay teapot again. She poured another cup.

I couldn't live through another cup. But I couldn't refuse it either. I took the cup in my hands and stood. Then I pointed to the shelves and started wandering among them as though I knew what I wanted.

Most of the canisters along the wall were made of tin, illustrated with scenes of traditional Japanese life. Some had the long made-up faces of kabuki actors. Others depicted rice paddies and farmers carrying poles with buckets of water suspended from each end. Still others showed castles, and men on horseback charging into battle. But one canister in the middle of the store depicted nothing. It was a sphere made of some porous rock like basalt. I knew that the tea in this canister must be especially precious and bitter to merit such a container.

I took it off the shelf and noted how heavy it felt. I looked on all sides for a price tag but found none. I imagined how impressed Chizuko and her father would be if I gave them this. How quickly they'd forgive me for my rudeness.

But then another thought came to me. Maybe I was being too sensitive, rather than not sensitive enough. Maybe the humiliation I thought I'd visited on Chizuko and her father was in my imagination. After all, neither had said anything. Maybe I was just a curious *gaijin* to them.

I didn't know what to think anymore. My stomach hurt and I couldn't swallow another drop of this tea. I looked behind me and saw that the old woman had stepped into the back room again. Quickly, I lifted the lid from the sphere and poured the tea inside. I closed the lid just as the woman returned.

I hoped she hadn't seen me. How would I explain that? Pouring her best tea into a new batch would be the ultimate rudeness.

For a moment, she looked at me, bewildered.

"*Ikura desuka?*" I asked. I had planned all along to buy it. But obviously, I couldn't give it to Chizuko or her father now. I'd have to take it home with me as a keepsake, this soggy tea. At least the container was pretty. For that reason, I knew it could cost a hundred dollars or more. I prepared myself.

The woman covered her face with her hands. I thought she was crying. Maybe she *had* seen me pour the tea away. Then she took her hands away and I saw she was laughing. She laughed for a good minute, and then she said, "You can't buy that. That's my husband."

What could I do but replace him? Who knows how long he'd sat there on the shelf undisturbed, until some crazy *gaijin* came in and poured tea over him? Of course, I'd seen the Japanese offer rice crackers and sake on the graves of their loved ones, but I'd never known the spirits to drink so directly.

I'm sure my eyes betrayed me because the woman bit her finger and tried not to laugh. She approached me then and looked at me almost maternally, almost fondly. But I backed out the door.

I felt another pang in my side. Excruciating. I thought it was from the tea. Then another pain came even sharper. I spun around, unaware of the direction of my suffering. It had started on my side and spread through my body. Across the way, I saw the giant crab, motionless now. Two men sat against the closed grating of the store, sharing a smoke. They watched me intently. I took two steps away from them, toward the bridge, clutching my side. Something exploded inside me. I staggered and fell on my back.

Presently, I saw the faces of the two men hovering above me. They looked more curious than concerned. I thought I recognized them as two of the men I'd seen begging listlessly on the bridge. Or the man on the train. Or Chizuko's father. "Could you sell me a coach-class ticket on the Bullet Train to Tokyo?" I asked them deliriously. This was one of the first things I'd memorized from my list of helpful Japanese phrases.

They exchanged looks and one of them broke away. To find out if the Bullet Train was full, I supposed. I'd settle for first class, I wanted to tell them, but couldn't manage. My mouth felt dry and bitter. I thought I was dying.

Actually, my appendix had ruptured. Of course, I didn't find that out until I awoke in the hospital. Lying there in the middle of Shinsaibashi, I had no idea. I thought this had happened because I couldn't even master the rudiments of polite behavior. I thought I was the first *gaijin* ever to die of culture shock. Then the old woman from the tea shop came into my view. She knelt down beside me, cradling my head in her arms. She was offering me something to drink. I didn't want to. No, I wouldn't. I wouldn't drink her tea. I wouldn't swallow her dead husband. No, not that. All I wanted was a ride on the Bullet Train. Any class would do. All I wanted was to get out of the way of the mechanical crab with its crazy swinging arms. The woman whispered something softly to me, something mildly chiding, and offered me the cup again. I saw then that her hair was on fire, but all I could do was gawk at the flames that surrounded but wouldn't consume her.

She offered me the cup again, and this time, I gave in. And what I tasted wasn't hot and bitter, but cool and sweet. I couldn't believe it. I nearly cried. It tasted like milk and honey. It tasted like something they'd give you as a reward, like something to calm you after a long and difficult journey.

WERNHER VON BRAUN'S LAST PICNIC

"YOUR CAT'S A RETARD," Cheryl says. "He's always provoking Pandora."

Cheryl's constantly using words like *retard* even though she knows better. She's studying for a master's in psychology and working as a counselor at a drug intervention center called Comeback. Cheryl says the center has a 99-percent failure rate, and is staffed with counselors more cynical than herself. Still, Comeback turns a profit and has a mile-long waiting list, mostly because the parents of these kids have nothing else to do with them. At least the center is aptly named. Everyone eventually returns for more treatment.

"You're a regular hooligan," I tell Wernher, and toast him with the beer I've been trying to relax with.

Wernher, the drooping fat sacks on his stomach swishing, pads across the room toward me and Cheryl. Cheryl's cat, Pandora, sitting placidly in the middle of the living room, makes a low moan as Wernher crosses her path. Pandora's moan is like Japanese koto music, a single string plucked to a sour crescendo. After nine months, she still loathes Wernher, probably because Wernher never learned cat etiquette, never studied the protocol of territory, grooming, and litter-box maintenance. He doesn't even understand hisses or yowls.

"Really, Rick," Cheryl says, picking up Pandora, who squirms to be set free. "We should do something with him. I just don't feel comfortable around that cat."

"What do you mean, do something?" I say. "What's there to do? Enroll him in a class for the learning deficient? Maybe he should pick up a valuable skill and become a productive member of society. For God's sake, he's a cat. By nature, they're simple-minded."

"Not like Wernher," Cheryl says. "Pandora's not like Wernher."

"Oh sorry, I forgot. The cat genius. The Siamese princess."

Pandora, who's been struggling for the last minute to be put down, finally succeeds in breaking out of Cheryl's arms. Instead of going anywhere important, she just sits next to Cheryl. Then she looks at me and closes her eyes with two measured blinks, like some kind of code. I blink back, but she just turns her head.

"Your behavior's aberrant, Rick," Cheryl says, apparently noticing what I thought was a private exchange.

"Besides," I say, "Wernher's not my cat."

Cheryl does the whole routine: a sigh, a look at the ceiling, a wrinkled nose, a click of the tongue. She often uses this portfolio of looks when one of her cronies from Comeback calls to gossip about a client: "Yeah, drug dealing has made Jimmy a real pillar of society. He didn't even know how to *count* in high school, but now he's got his metric system down, doesn't he?"

"You really think Michelle's going to pick up Wernher someday?" she says.

"I didn't say that."

"But you'd like her to stop by, wouldn't you?" She says this coolly, like I'm a client and she has no stake in the matter.

"I didn't say that."

Cheryl gives me a flat look and blinks like Pandora did. That look is enough to completely confuse me. I don't even know what we're talking about anymore.

This is the way arguing with her always goes. Like playing chess with someone who seems completely logical. Then, halfway through the game, she starts playing by the rules of checkers, bunny-hopping around the board with one of her pawns.

"I'm afraid I can't help you with this one," she says. "This is an issue you need to resolve for yourself without any help from me."

"You mean, interference."

"Attitude," she scolds, doubly cool. "If you didn't want my help, then why did you bring up the issue?"

"You're the one who's been talking about how dumb Wernher is," I say.

"That's not the point," she says.

Whatever the point is, I don't think I want to know. One of the problems between us is that there's always some point to be made. Why can't it be enough to sit here drinking beer in our apartment in the afternoon, listening to music and ignoring both of our dumb cats?

"Come here, Wernher," I say, leaning forward and holding out my hand as though I have a treat. As soon as the cat sees some attention being proffered, he thumps over, bounds onto my lap, and collapses into an ecstatic heap.

Cheryl stands with Pandora as though Wernher's mere presence is deadly to them both.

Wernher, though, doesn't even notice the rebuff. He curls his head into my lap and purrs loudly.

Cheryl starts across the living room toward the bedroom.

"You're all wound up and you're making me tense," she tells me.

"You made *me* tense!" I yell after her. "What am I supposed to do with Wernher then? He's at least ten years old. No one's going to want a cat that old. As far as I know, there aren't any retirement homes for cats either."

"That's not the issue," Cheryl says, turning around, glaring.

Maybe I don't understand the point, but I grasp the issue. The issue, of course, is Michelle. I shift Wernher, who flops on his back, purring louder, his tongue stuck between his teeth.

Michelle and I found Wernher after a movie. We were walking to a bar when Wernher crossed our path. Michelle, who's a cat lover, called him over and petted him, and then we continued on our walk. The cat started following us. We kept on walking. We walked over a mile and the cat followed us the whole way. Finally, Michelle and I decided to stop into a bar. I held the door open for her and I held the door open for the cat. He ran inside. Michelle and I took seats up at the front of the bar, and Wernher rubbed against our legs. The bartender filled up a shot glass of milk for the cat. The cat drank the milk, then cleaned himself as Michelle and I talked. We were at that point in our relationship when we had to decide where we were headed. But we didn't talk about that, though it was on our minds. We talked about the cat, how smart he was.

When we left the bar, the cat followed us outside and all the way back home. I was the one who named him. I named him Wernher after the rocket scientist Wernher von Braun. I guess that made Wernher as much my cat as Michelle's, but she was always the one who fed him and gave him attention.

I get up to follow Cheryl down the hall, and the phone rings. It's probably one of Cheryl's clients, but with my luck it'll be Michelle. She told me she was going to pick up Wernher sometime, but she hasn't been in touch since the day she moved out, and I don't even know her address. Now would not be a good time for her to call and that's why it must be her.

I stand in the doorway of the bedroom while Cheryl dumps Pandora on the bed and picks up the phone. It's Scott, one of Cheryl's coworkers at Comeback. Apparently, Jimmy, one of their clients, ripped off Scott's bike.

"Was it locked?" Cheryl says.

I hear some angry noise from the phone, then Cheryl interrupts. "Did he tell anyone where he was headed?"

Cheryl's silent for a moment, then says, "Right. More power to him. We'll just wait for the cops to drag him back, then we'll kick his ass out on the street. Maybe if we're lucky, the cops will just take him out. Make our lives easier. Gee, maybe we should have been bounty hunters instead of counselors, don't you think?"

Cheryl listens, then laughs and says, "Right, more rewarding. I guess we missed our calling. Oh well. Keep me posted."

Cheryl gets off the phone and looks at me as though I'm some new client she's never seen before, and I've just barged in without an appointment.

"What?" she says.

"I just . . ." I say.

"You just what?" she demands.

I don't know what I'm going to say, but I blurt out, "I just don't know what you're angry for. It's not my fault."

She looks at me and yells, "What's not your fault? Did I say anything was your fault? You don't make any sense."

Wernher appears between my legs and scoots into the room as though he's been invited. He jumps up on the bed. Pandora springs up, yowling resentfully. Before Wernher has a chance to settle in, Cheryl grabs him off the bed and thrusts him in my arms. "Here, take your girlfriend's retarded cat and get out. I don't want to see him again. Understand, Rick?" She speaks slowly, like I don't know English. "Do . . . you . . . un-der-stand?"

"*Ex*-girlfriend!" I yell. "She's my ex-girlfriend."

With one hand I grasp Wernher, who's dug his claws into my chest, and with the other hand I slam the door. From the other side, I scream at her, "What's up your butt, huh?" But she doesn't answer and eventually I leave.

"Crowd?" Wernher keeps asking from beneath the lid of the picnic basket I've got him in.

"Seems like we're finally getting a break in the weather," the cabbie tells me. "Looks like you've got an unhappy cat, though." Though? Like the cat and the weather are connected? He's a guy about my age with a giant mustache and a blue beret.

"You know anyone who wants a cat?" I say, my last-ditch effort.

"Not me," the man says. "I hate cats. Matter of fact, hate's too soft a word for it. I abhor them."

"Why?" I ask. "Did you have a bad experience with a cat once?"

Wernher tries to lift the lid off the basket. He succeeds in sticking his head out a little. He gives me a terrified look and I stroke his chin, saying, "Shh, it's not so bad, Wernher."

"Why do some people hate dogs?" the cabbie asks. "Call it prejudice. I didn't grow up with them. My folks had one when I was born and my mom caught it about to pounce on me in my crib. But I don't remember that. I guess you could say I'm a cat bigot. I buy all those dead-cat books, though. I mean, for light entertainment," he says, turning around. "When I want something of substance, I head straight for Kafka." He laughs, and hits the steering wheel with a fist. "Franz, the man, the myth, the motion picture!"

"Let me out here," I say.

"We're not at the shelter yet."

"I know. I want out."

This cabbie never even owned a cat, and he hates them. I wish I could buy a dead-cabdriver book. Cheryl doesn't even know Michelle, and she hates her. I can't even mention Michelle around Cheryl. And Michelle . . . The equation doesn't fit here. Michelle at least knew me well enough to decide that she hated me. If people could dump each other at shelters, there'd only be room for humans in those cages. Wernher. He doesn't know any of this. He doesn't even know his name is Wernher von Braun. All he knows is that he's in a cramped dark space, where cats sometimes like to be, but usually of their own choice.

I walk down the street and try to keep the basket from swinging too much. Wernher's got his claws out. They make a scratching sound on the bottom of the basket as he tries not to slide around. I almost need to use both hands to manage the basket. As I shove past the other pedestrians, they look at me as if wondering where I could be off to in such a hurry. Some emergency picnic perhaps.

Instead of heading for the shelter, a right turn at Fullerton, I turn left, toward the lake. The lakefront. A park. I open the picnic basket. Wernher has peed in the bottom and his fur is wet. He's crouched in his pee, staring up at the light. He opens his mouth, but no sound comes out. I let him out of the basket. He isn't sure where he is, and stands uncertainly on the grass, then starts eating it blade by blade. "Crowd?" he says over and over. I look out over the water. It's a fine sunny day. A few sailboats on the lake. An overdressed elderly man, bundled up with scarf and overcoat even though it's June, sits on a bench. A couple cuts across the grass.

I want him to run away, but Wernher wouldn't stand a chance out here. I stretch out on the grass, getting eye level with him. He looks at me sideways while gnawing on a piece of grass. Then he stops and nuzzles my chin, and I say, "Wernher, I wish you wouldn't do that. I wish you'd see it my way. I know that none of this is your fault."

"Crowd?" he says, and nuzzles me again.

"I know," I say. "I don't know what I want. That's worse than knowing what you want and being wrong, isn't it? Sometimes in the morning, I sit on the edge of the bed and watch Cheryl sleep. I look at her five minutes, ten, fifteen, until she wakes up. And then I say, 'How'd you sleep? Have any interesting dreams?' But that's not what I mean. What I really want to talk about is this: the idea that somewhere in the world there's exactly the right person for you. I want to ask her if she believes this, if she thinks it's more than just intersections of circumstance. Sometimes, I think about how in this particular city I fell in love with Michelle and then Cheryl, and in another city I never would have met either one."

Wernher doesn't say anything this time, but blinks twice and goes back to eating his grass. I feel something fall on my back and turn around quickly. The old man who's bundled up stands above me, not more than two feet away, shelling peanuts and letting them drop around him. He seems engrossed in what I've been saying to Wernher.

"I live with my only daughter and her husband," he tells me sadly, as though I asked him, and then he drops a shell by my feet and walks back to his bench.

I almost expect to see Michelle waiting in the apartment when I get home. I imagine that today is the day she's decided to pick Wernher up, and Cheryl has let her in. I imagine the two women seated on the couch together, exchanging notes about me. But no, the apartment's dark. Cheryl's nowhere to be found.

The phone rings, and when I answer it, I can tell that something's wrong. It's Scott. He sounds out of breath, weak. There's a flutter in his voice.

"Where's Cheryl?" he says.

"What do you mean?" I say. "Isn't she with you?"

"It's Jimmy," Scott says, and I think, Jimmy, Jimmy.

"Oh, the drug dealer," I say, relieved. "The little reprobate who stole—"

"My bike," he says. "I didn't lock it. I always lock it."

Slowly, he tells me what happened. It takes him nearly ten minutes, but I'm patient. I listen. Our phone cord is too short for me to do anything but stand in one place, though it's getting dark and I'd like to turn on a light. But I can't interrupt Scott. I can't be that callous. I can't say, "Scott, I'd like to hear you pour out your heart. I'd like to relieve your guilt, but it's getting dark and I'm hungry." The picnic basket is by my feet, and smells strongly of urine. I kick it away, but not far enough, not nearly. Soon, the whole apartment will reek.

"Yes, I'll tell her," I say when Scott finishes. And we say good-bye. Pandora sits beside me licking her foot pads and washing her face, then scurries off to the kitchen. A moment later, I hear her hop onto the kitchen counter.

I don't turn on a light immediately. Instead, I stand there with my head cocked as though I might hear some music. I *have* heard something, though I'm not sure what it is. It sounds like an old street vendor's cry. It's faint and comes from outside.

"Wernher!" someone's calling. "Wern-her!"

I go to the front window. Cheryl stands down below, near a street lamp. She wears a sweat suit. The wind blows her hair, and she tries to keep it back. No one else is on the street, and I still haven't turned on a light, so she doesn't know I'm here.

"Wernher!" she calls. I listen to her calling his name, unsure of what I'll do now. I realize I can't tell her that Jimmy, the boy she always said she hated, is dead.

I open the window and call down to her.

"I've been searching everywhere for him," she says, looking up. "I've gone through the closets, the drawers. I'm so worried."

"What do you mean?" I ask.

"Maybe he's trapped somewhere and can't get out," she says.

"What do you care?" I say.

She looks at me as though I've just spoken nonsense.

I give up. I go downstairs to help her search for Wernher, in all the alleyways, beside the garbage cans, in all those places a frightened cat might hide. But I know that searching is useless.

Still, we continue to hunt, and to keep up our spirits, we talk about posters, rewards, the loving new home that we're sure Wernher has lucked into. Eventually, we'll have to talk about Jimmy, and she'll wonder whether she was to blame, and I'll say, "No, of course not," and put my arms around her, and listen to her tell me stories of how horrible Jimmy was, and why she's just wasting her tears. But I won't believe her.

Eventually, we'll have to talk about us and what we did to Wernher. The picnic basket sits in the living room, the apartment is filling up with its smell. When Cheryl asks me about it, I'll stare at her and blink twice.

At the shelter, I had to fill out a form about the cat, whether it was a stray or a house cat, and why I was giving it up. The woman who gave me the form didn't glare at me with an accusing look. In fact, she seemed completely blasé. "You can leave that line blank if you want," she said when she saw I was having trouble explaining the cat's relationship to me.

After completing the form, I lifted him out of the picnic basket and cradled him in my arms. Immediately, he started purring, too trusting to even stay terrified, and I handed him over to the woman with the forms.

"How long do you keep them?" I asked.

"He's an old cat," she said, taking him from me. She picked

him up under his front legs, and he hung in front of her, his legs dangling. He looked like he was making a parachute drop.

In the morning, I'll go down to the shelter and wait for it to open, hoping that it's not too late. But for now, I go ahead and let Cheryl search for him, and I search with her. We search like animals, the ones I've heard about all my life, the heroic and loyal kind, who make continental journeys, or wait patiently by empty railway stations, too dumb to love incompletely.

THE LIBERATION
OF ROME

A YOUNG WOMAN NAMED AMY BULERIC sat in my office looking down at her feet. I figured someone had died, or maybe she
was having emotional problems, or was sick. I bolstered myself for
whatever horror or misfortune she might throw my way. A colleague
of mine forces students to bring in obituaries when they claim a rela-
tive has died, but I think that's pathetic. I'd rather believe a student
and risk being a fool than become power-crazed. So I was bolster-
ing myself because I was afraid to hear what Amy Buleric was going
to tell me about the reason for her absence for the last three weeks.
In my twenty-one years here, I've been told by just such shy and
diffident students all sorts of tales of personal tragedy—nearly anything you can imagine. To me, these frail shell-shocked students
appearing in my office are not con men and women seeking

extensions on their papers, but refugees from battle. I listen and give them any comfort I can. I try not to judge them. My critics would charge I am the inventor of the benefit of the doubt. They would tell you that I have created a welfare state of "Incompletes." But where is compassion these days? If one or two students take advantage of my trust, that's their problem. My course in "The Last Days of Rome" means nothing compared to what some of these kids have gone through. One time, a student sent me a note: "Dr. Radlisch, I'm sorry I can't finish the paper on Hannibal for you." The next day, I learned the boy had killed himself—not because of my paper, of course. He had problems I only found out about later. He must have sent me that note out of a pitiful sense of duty. Still, his words haunt me even today.

This young woman was fidgety, not looking at me, and so I sat there patiently, waiting for her to find the courage to tell me whatever it was that bothered her. As I waited, I regarded her with a kind of bored desire, not actual lust, nothing really predatory, but a feeble cousin to lust—a kind of respectful admiration. Amy wore her reddish blonde hair in ringlets that cascaded about her face and nearly completely hid her small ears. She was a delicate girl, and at first I thought, An eating disorder? But her complexion was too ruddy, her eyes too bright. She wore a summery dress, and silver bangles everywhere, on one of her ankles just above her leather sandal, even a banglelike ornament around her neck. I fixed my gaze on that neck, the blonde hairs in disarray nearly invisible against the skin. At times like this, when I have nothing to do but study the students, I sometimes imagine them collapsing into my arms with a weeping admission: "Dr. Radlisch, I have always loved you!" And me, bewildered but responsive: "Yes, Susan, Betty, James, Tim, Gretta, Roger . . . Oh, Roger, I know, but this is foolishness!"

"Dr. Radlisch," she said finally, her voice a whisper.

"Take your time, Amy," I said, just as softly.

She looked past me to one of my bookshelves. "Why do you have that sign in your office?"

I sat up and turned around so quickly that a muscle popped in my neck. The sign was hand-lettered, done by a friend of my daughter's who specializes in calligraphy for weddings. It reads, "If Rome be weak, where shall strength be found?"

"It's a quote from the poet Lucan," I said.

"Yes, I know," she said, her bangled arm sweeping aside her hair. She looked at me with what seemed suddenly like defiance and contempt. "But why is it here? It's . . . like . . . propaganda."

"I'm not sure I understand what you're saying, Amy," I said. I sat back in my chair. I lost sight of her neck. My thoughts, my voice became formal. "I thought we were here to discuss your absences, any problems you've been having."

I saw she was about to cry, so I stopped. "I mean," I said, softening my voice, "it's hard to find a solution unless I know what's wrong. Still, I'm glad you stopped in here to talk. I hate it when students simply disappear without a word."

It was too late. She started to cry, and I could see this was the last thing she wanted to do, that she was terribly embarrassed. The tears ran down her face and she didn't make any move to wipe them away. She just clenched her teeth and mumbled something, probably a curse for breaking down in front of me. I fumbled for a tissue in my desk, and finally found one, but when I looked at her again, I saw that she'd stopped, that her face didn't even look tear-stained. Her eyes were still moist, but that was all. She looked at me with a fierce expression, a hand touching the bangle around her throat as though I had just tried to choke her.

"I wanted to disappear," she said, "but I couldn't. I had to confront you. That sign is my problem. Part of it anyway."

"Confront me?" I said. I scooted my chair back an inch or two.

"You've probably never had someone like me in one of your classes, and so there was no one to challenge your ideas."

"Ms. Buleric," I said. "I teach Roman history. I don't know what you're talking about. I have no ideas to be challenged. The writings of the ancients. I voice their ideas with my tongue. Not their ideas. Their accounts. I'm not sure where this is all leading, but I thought we were here to talk about your absences."

"I am here to talk about your lies," she said.

I stood up. Amy Buleric didn't rise from her chair and leave, as I expected she would. I have had paranoid students, ones who came to my office and rambled and made little sense. I have had disruptive, smart-aleck students who, when I mentioned Caligula, whinnied like a horse. I have had students who refused to learn, who were apathetic, angry at their parents, sick of society, drug-addicted, TV-addled. I have had stupid students, smelly students, cheating, doubtful, sinful students. But the only students who thought I had any ideas to challenge were the pious students, the fundamentalists who thought I should spend the entire semester discussing the persecution of the Christians, or the parents of these students, who on occasion called to condemn me for inculcating their children with "paganist values." Amy Buleric seemed to belong to this last group, and if she was one of their number, then I was going to become very irritated with her. Here I'd thought she needed my sympathy, my help, and she'd only come to accuse me of telling lies.

I sat on the edge of my desk and folded my arms. "How old are you, Amy? Nineteen? Twenty?"

"Twenty," she said.

"Why are you here?" I asked.

"Someone needs to stop you from telling lies."

I waved my hand at her. "Not that. I mean, why are you in college?" I smiled to show I wasn't her enemy. "Do you feel that you know everything already? Or do you think that college might just possibly, just on an outside chance, teach you something, something that might even challenge some of your old notions, or the notions of your parents?"

"What about you, Dr. Radlisch?" she said, sitting up straight in her chair. "Do you know everything already? What about your old notions? Can they be challenged?"

"People say I'm open-minded," I said, glancing at my watch.

"I'm here to better my people," she said, looking around the office as though her people had gathered around her.

"Your people? Are you a Mormon?"

"No."

"You're not . . . I mean, you don't look . . ."

"I'm a Vandal, Dr. Radlisch."

I put my chin in my hand. "A vandal," was all I could manage to say.

"Part Vandal," she said. "Over half."

"You deface property?" I said.

"Another lie," she said. "Another stinking Roman lie." She spat on my carpet.

"You spat on my carpet," I told her, and pointed to it.

"I'm a Vandal, Dr. Radlisch," she said. "If you only knew the truth about us."

"Amy," I said calmly. "I'm not doubting you, of course. But what you're telling me is that you're a Vandal. V-A-N-D-A-L. Vandal. Like the tribe? The one that disappeared from history in the sixth century when Belisarius defeated them and sold them into slavery?"

"Pig," she said. "Dog. Roman dung. Belisarius." And she spat again.

"Please stop spitting on my carpet," I asked her.

She nodded, and folded her arms primly in her lap.

"And you're here in my office to set the record straight," I said.

"There isn't any record, Dr. Radlisch," she said. "That's the point. The Vandal tradition is entirely oral. We don't trust the written word. That was the way of the Romans. 'Lies are the province of Romans and writers.' That's an old Vandal proverb. The only record you have is the record of the Romans. They tell you that we were a warlike people who invaded Gaul at the beginning of the fifth century. But that was only because the Huns attacked us first. They drove us out of the Baltic. And we didn't attack the Gauls. We were just defending ourselves! Then the Franks defeated us in 409 and we fled into Spain. We were only there twenty years when a lying Roman governor invited us into North Africa to establish an independent homeland on the ashes of Carthage. We should have known better than to set up camp in Carthage. The only reason we captured Rome was to stop their oppression of us and other peoples they had colonized or destroyed. We didn't sack Rome. We liberated it."

She knew her history. Or at least a version, one that I had never heard before.

"And now you're coming forward."

"We've always been here," she said. "You've never noticed."

I wanted to believe her, but I was having a little difficulty. "So for the last fourteen hundred years . . ."

"That's right," she said. "Oh, we've intermarried some, but we've kept our traditions alive." She started to wail. Not a wail exactly. A high-pitched but guttural sound like someone retching. Her eyes were closed and her mouth was stretched in an unnatural grimace. After a minute of this, she stopped, opened her eyes, and wiped her brow.

"Birth song," she announced.

"It's very different," I said. "Haunting."

She seemed pleased that I'd said this. She bowed her head. "For over a millennium, our voices have been silenced. No one wanted to hear the Vandal songs. No one cared, though I suppose we were lucky. In some ways, we prefer the world's indifference to its attention. As soon as you're recognized, you're hunted and destroyed. So we waited. And now we're back."

My shoulders tensed and I rubbed my neck where the muscle had popped.

"Thank you for coming forward," I told her. "I know how hard it must be for you. I'm sure there are many things you could teach me."

She smiled at me again and all the anger seemed to be gone. "About the paper that's due?" she said.

"What?"

"'Lies are the province of Romans and writers.'"

At first I didn't get it, but then I saw what she was telling me. "Oh, right," I said. "I guess you can't write it, can you?"

"No, I'm sorry," she said.

"No, don't be sorry," I said, reaching over and nearly touching her shoulder, but not quite. "I understand. I understand completely. It's part of your tradition."

"The Vandal tradition," she said. "Thanks, Dr. Radlisch. I knew you'd understand."

"That's my middle name."

"It is?"

"No, Amy. It's just a turn of phrase."

"Oh," she said, and smiled. She liked me now. I could tell.

But I felt saddened. I was so used to teaching my subject in a certain way. I had found a strange comfort in Lucan's quote, but now his question seemed unanswerable, at least by me. "Where shall strength be found?" How was I going to learn the new ways?

That night, I dreamed about my student who had killed himself. He was accusing me of something. He told me I was going to flunk out. I panicked and shot him. That was the dream. Ludicrous, but when I awoke, it felt so real that I nearly cried with relief. When I went to my office that day, I almost expected to see graffiti scrawled on the walls: "Death to all Vandals!" But there was none. The walls were clean. No one had defaced them. What's more, Amy never showed up in class again. Beside her name on the final transcript, there was simply a blank, no "Withdrawn" as I'd hoped. It was up to me. I didn't know what to do. I couldn't give her an A. But I couldn't flunk her. She knew her history. So I settled on a B. But why had she stopped coming to class? Was it me? I thought we understood one another now. As I always told my students, they should come see me, no matter what the problem, before they just disappeared.

THE PERFECT WORD

DESPITE DR. FISCHER'S ANISE-SCENTED BREATH, he had, overall, a flat unlaundered smell—surprising for a man who wore a crisp suit with a silk tie, and whose thin hair was slick and parted in the middle. The trim fingernails, the closely shaven face, the speckless eyeglasses didn't fit a man whose last bath might have been in the forties or fifties. Maybe he pressed his clothes without washing them. Or somehow ironed without removing them. I had once read that Archduke Ferdinand died at Sarajevo because he had his clothes stitched to his body and the doctors couldn't cut the layers of regal wear off fast enough to attend to his wounds. Perhaps that isn't true, but it wouldn't be the first time self-mutilation and fashion overlapped.

I saw Dr. Fischer all the time where I worked, a patisserie and coffee shop called The Runcible Spoon. At the time, I was studying video at the Art Institute and working twenty-five hours a week, hoping to save up my money to move, either to New York or L.A. I hadn't made up my mind. Fischer came in regularly and sat alone in a corner bent over papers. None of us had an inkling what they were, and I didn't ask. He gave no indication that he remembered who I was, and why should he? I'd taken one class from him when I was full-time at Northwestern. Chinese calligraphy. I hadn't shown much talent. I had handled the brush like a first-grader using a fat pencil. My strokes came out thick when I wanted them thin and anemic when I wanted them bold. I'd volunteered to run the slide projector that semester, and for this Fischer had given me an A. I couldn't think of any other reason. Even though most students considered Fischer too cerebral, they still liked him for being easygoing. The truth was, if he remembered your name, you got an A. If he didn't, he'd give you a B.

The staff at The Runcible Spoon called him Mr. Raisin or, alternatively, Mr. Crispy, because he always ordered "Raisin toast, extra crispy." No matter how many times I waited on him, he always gave me the same instructions, as though I was waiting on him for the first time. So it surprised me one day when he called me by name over to his table and started talking to me about his work as though we were old buddies.

"What do you think, Rick?" he said, pointing with a nubby pencil to an onionskin manuscript. "Do you think *liaison* is a better word than *rendezvous*? These are two country boys going fishing." He looked up at me with his frank eyes and touched the eraser of his pencil to a front tooth.

I didn't really know what he was talking about and I couldn't imagine two country boys having a fishing liaison. "Do they speak French?" I asked.

"No, no, they speak Chinese, of course," he said, rapping the pencil twice on the tabletop. "But that hardly matters. These are translations. Now which is it? Rendezvous or liaison?"

Fischer sat back in his chair and stared at me. I had other customers waiting and it really didn't matter to me which word he used. I just wanted to choose the one that would make him leave me the bigger tip.

"Rendezvous," I said firmly, and saw something fall in his eyes. "Maybe liaison," I said.

"Are you sure?" he asked. He took a sip of espresso, then set the cup down and began furiously erasing a word on the onionskin paper.

In the next half-hour, things started to get pretty frantic around the restaurant, and I was run from one corner to the next trying to satisfy the demands of all my customers at once. Why couldn't my boss schedule enough people for our rushes? That's all I wanted to know. He knew when the rushes were, and at that moment the place was full, and only two of us were working out front: myself and Gina, who had the counter and the register. And of course, almost every customer thought that every other customer didn't exist. When it comes to refills, customers, as a lot, can be pretty solipsistic. I almost poured my whole coffeepot on one woman who was getting antsy about her strudel and Kona refill.

"Rick, we're eighty-sixing the strudel," Gina confided as she swooshed by me. "I'm making some more Kona and we're out of cups."

"Is this your first day as a waiter?" the woman asked me.

I managed to control myself, and dashed to the kitchen and gathered a rack of empty cups. The machine looked like a huge breadbox. It had sliding doors on two sides, one for putting dishes in, the other for removing them. I slid the tray in, pushed a button, and stood back. At first, the machine made a grinding noise, then I heard the sound of rushing water, and steam rose from the cracks of the sliding doors. The steam settled and the grinding halted.

This was what we called "the deception cycle." You had to pay attention with this machine or you could scald yourself pretty bad. Suddenly, steam rose again from the cracks and surrounded me. The water rushed and the rattling was twice as loud.

Gina and I did a kind of ballet out front. I traded her the tray of cups for a pot of freshly brewed Kona. An arm shot out and grabbed me by the elbow.

I dropped the coffeepot and it shattered by my feet. Everyone swiveled around. I regarded the person who had caused me to drop the coffeepot. It was Dr. Fischer, and he sat frozen in his chair, his pencil poised by his ear.

I looked down. The coffee had sprayed all over his pant legs. I hadn't heard him scream, and he didn't make any movements of discomfort now either.

"I hope I didn't cause you to do that," he said.

"Abandon hope," I told him, and turned to get a mop.

When I returned, I gave him a clean dishtowel, for which he thanked me abundantly. "*Liaison* was the perfect word," he added. "You're not familiar with Chinese idiom, are you?"

He spoke with a thick German accent, actually Austrian, but I understood the nuances of European speech about as well as I knew Chinese. Fischer seemed like an odd combination. "I am not Chinese," he'd announced the first day of class, enunciating each word in his severe accent, like a German prison guard. This drew a laugh from the students. "I was born in Shanghai in 1930, where my father was the Austrian consul general. I was raised there until the Japanese invaded in 1937. I thought I'd explain this to you early on. Otherwise, you might think I was Chinese, and I certainly do not want to confuse anyone." And this brought another laugh.

"What are you working on?" I asked, leaning on my mop. It wasn't that I was interested in what he was doing, though I had been curious in the past. But I was also keenly aware that the woman who'd asked me if this was my first day was staring at me. Let the coffee-addled barbarian go into withdrawal, I thought. I didn't know why I was still working at the restaurant. I'd been thinking about the Peace Corps lately.

"Poems from the Tang dynasty," he said. He smiled up at me with a set of teeth that didn't look brushed. A black seed was wedged between his two top front teeth.

"Let me tell you a secret," he said. "All these years, Westerners have been reading fakes. Not the real poems by the real men. No one knows the way these men really were but me."

"Sounds great," I said.

I was about to ask him if he wanted some more raisin toast, my cue to him that I was no longer his student but his waiter. Some customers, not just ex-profs, forget you're not there to listen to them, and have to be politely reminded.

I felt someone tap me on the shoulder. I turned. It was the woman who'd asked me if this was my first day. She carried her coffee cup in front of her like a beggar. "Am I expected to wait all day?" she asked.

Instead of answering her, I sat down at the table with Dr. Fischer. He shuffled his papers out of my way.

"Hey," the woman said, rapping her cup on my shoulder blade. I pointed to the sign above the register, which read, "If you're in a hurry, you're in the wrong place."

She turned around and walked over to Gina at the register, who gave me a drowning look. I felt sorry for Gina, but I couldn't help it. Sometimes, you have to make a stand against customers.

The next day, I received a call from Dr. Fischer inviting me over to his apartment for lunch. He was acting mysteriously, saying he had something important to discuss with me, something about yesterday, and he didn't want to talk about it over the phone. He whispered like the phone was tapped. I didn't have anything better to do, so I said sure I'd come to lunch, and took the El from my apartment in Wicker Park to the Loop, changed trains to the Howard, and changed again in Evanston. From my stop in Evanston, I walked about ten blocks to the lakefront apartment where Fischer lived.

We ate in Dr. Fischer's dining room. The lunch consisted mainly of Korean pickles the colors of Christmas ornaments. This was a pickle sampler—reds, greens, and oranges cut in every shape from julienne to spears.

After lunch, Fischer produced a folder and spread out the contents on the table: a stack of papers, some written in English, some in Chinese. He told me to look them over.

I didn't know Chinese. I had no idea which translations matched the originals, but I pretended to know, glancing back and forth between them. Even though I couldn't read the characters, I knew a little bit about them. I recognized the simplest characters, the ones for mountain, river, sun, man, and woman.

One of Dr. Fischer's manx cats, Vanessa, jumped on the dining table and flopped down on the papers. "Oh well, we can work later," Dr. Fischer said. It didn't seem to occur to him to move the cat. The other cat, Sophie, rubbed up against a table leg. Dr. Fischer had introduced them to me the moment I'd walked in.

We went into the living room, where the walls were covered with scrolls and paintings and framed calligraphy. I sat down on a brocaded couch and Dr. Fischer took out his checkbook and started to write a check.

I recognized one of the calligraphic styles on the wall from Dr. Fischer's slide lectures. The strokes were thin and long and delicate. The lines were straight and unwavering. Black lines frozen or plucked perfectly from thin air. They seemed created by someone who understood absolutes, who knew the distance and length of infinity. They had been done by the Chinese emperor Hui-tsung, who devoted all of his time and money to the arts in his kingdom. As Dr. Fischer had explained in class, the arts had flourished under the emperor, but he neglected everything else, including his military. Eventually, barbarians overran the country, capturing Hui-tsung and bringing about the end of the Northern Sung dynasty. The barbarians imprisoned him in a dungeon, where he spent the rest of his life perfecting his writing style.

Fischer looked up at me and said, "So I gather you're willing to take on the task at hand?"

I leaned forward, resting my arms on my legs. Then I straightened up and sat back in the couch. "What exactly is it?"

"Translator," he said, blinking. "I thought you understood."

I put my hand to my chest. "But I don't know Chinese."

"Let me tell you a little bit more about my project," he said, and he put aside the checkbook, face up on the coffee table, which was an oval of glass supported by twisted limbs of polished black wood. I glanced at the amount, seventy-five dollars, written in a hand that was equal in beauty to the way Fischer made his Chinese characters. "The poems you've been reading are from the Tang dynasty," Dr. Fischer said. "They're among some of the most famous poems in Chinese. Poems by Li Po, Tu Fu, Po Chu-i." The *Po* of Li Po and Po Chu-i, he pronounced *Bye*. "Surprisingly, they've never been properly translated," he said. "Or rather, accurately translated. Do you know why that is? This might shock you."

I had no idea what he was talking about. But Dr. Fischer leaned forward and locked me with his eyes as though I understood completely, and was just playing dumb.

Dr. Fischer settled back in his chair. "Many of the Tang poets would take excursions to the country together, something like Chautauquas." Dr. Fischer must have seen the blank look on me because he rolled his hand in front of his face and added, "A conference, a get-together. You understand?"

"Would you like some anise seeds?" Fischer asked me. "They make a wonderful breath freshener." Fischer smiled, and dipped his hand into the bowl of anise seeds on the table. He tilted his head, opened his mouth, and trickled the seeds in. "What's bothering you?" he said after a moment.

"Nothing," I said. "I thought you might be bothered by the fact that I don't read or speak Chinese."

"Bothered?" Fischer said. "I'm delighted. If you knew a word of Chinese, I'd ask you to leave and bill you for lunch. Still, it's important for you to look at the originals. We must learn to respect the text even if we don't understand it."

Fischer grabbed the blue bowl of anise seeds and set it in front of me.

"Waley, Anderson, and the others," Dr. Fischer said. "They're little schoolgirls. Even contemporary Chinese scholars ignore the truth." He looked at me blankly, then opened his mouth wide, and a single sharp laugh burst out as if an animal had been trapped inside him. The laugh startled me and I dropped anise seeds on the coffee table. Fischer looked at them and waved his hand. He laughed again and I laughed, too.

"As in Greek society of the same time, love, spiritual and intellectual, was reserved for men, and the Tang poets, when they went away together, wrote love poems to each other. These are the poems that survive, but they have been bowdlerized." He squeezed one of his hands like he was getting milk from a cow's udder. "In some cases, the mistakes are innocent. We have to understand that the poets disguised the sex act in metaphor. It's obvious enough, but most translators choose not to see. A fish leaping, a musical instrument, the braiding of hair. And of course, there aren't any personal pronouns in Chinese, so who is to say the speaker is addressing a she instead of a he?"

I didn't have an answer for that, but then I'd only taken one semester of Chinese calligraphy.

"I have one more question," he said, craning his neck and regarding me solemnly. "You're not gay, are you?"

"Sorry," I said.

"Sorry?" he said. "Why apologize? You're much better off. And I prefer it this way." Still, he looked slightly disappointed.

He preferred that I didn't know Chinese. He preferred that I wasn't gay. He preferred that I didn't know anything about poetry. So what were my qualifications?

Fumbling with the folder of calligraphy, I closed it as though it were a criminal file on me.

"There's a mistake," I said.

"Where?" Dr. Fischer asked, leaning forward.

"I mean, between us," I said.

Fischer took a breath. "Undoubtedly. There always is."

"Maybe I'm not the person you want."

Fischer waved his hand like he was clearing smoke.

"Will seventy-five dollars do? Keep track of the time you spend on these and count up your hours. I'll pay you seventy-five dollars per hour, if you find that reasonable." His cat had left the dining-room table, and so he gathered up his translations in a manila folder and handed them to me.

An hour. Seventy-five dollars an hour. I reeled. "What do you want me to do?" I asked weakly.

"Make changes. Make lots of changes. I'll see you in a week," and he let me outside.

That night, I lined up a dozen translations on the kitchen table and read them through several times. They were attributed to twelve different poets from the Tang dynasty, but they all sounded alike. A typical one was by the poet Wang Chih-huan:

Waiting in Vain for My Friend Wu

Woodcutters go back and forth
with their saws
felling one another's stout timber.
The barbarian moonlight
excites upward-leaping fish
along the banks of the Ch'u River.
Twin hills swell wide—
Moans fill an orchid-wood boat.
And still, because you promised,
I wait,
plucking the one-stringed guitar.

The rest of the poems were even worse. There wasn't anything poetic about these translations. They were crude and laughable, and even if Fischer was correct, he should have left them the way they were. If people didn't want to see something, there was no way to force them to see it. One was titled "Wang Wei Remembers the Daisy Chain." Another one was called "Golden Showers at the Temple of Heaped Fragrance." The worst, though, was "In Farewell to Field Clerk Han Going Home: A Song of Bodily Fluids."

I studied the first poem but didn't have the faintest idea what I was supposed to do with it. Tentatively, I scratched out the word *excites*, and tried to think of a substitute. I wasn't sure why I didn't like the word. In fact, the more I looked at the word, the more it seemed just fine. Who was I to change around Dr. Fischer's words, even if I did think it was a stupid poem? I didn't respect the translation, much less the original.

I looked at the poem again. I wrote the word *gooses* in place of *excites*, then crossed that out and settled on *strokes*.

But whoever heard of ancient gay Chinese poetry? If what Fischer said was true, people would have known about it long before now. Maybe this whole project was a ruse. Maybe the old boy had a thing for me. A year earlier, a professor had shown up naked on the doorstep of one of his students in the middle of the night. He'd banged on her door and demanded a nightcap. The professor had been forced into early retirement. Things like this happened all the time.

Doesn't it bother you at all that he's stringing you along like this? I thought.

But he's paying me.

That was enough for one night. I put the poems away, and the next day I cashed Dr. Fischer's check.

Fischer led me to the dining room like he was a general and I was a scientist working on a top-secret project. Everything looked the same as before. The papers seemed untouched. The plates of food were still there as well, though browner and with a large cloud of fruit flies surrounding them.

"What are your suggestions?" he said.

"I don't have any," I said.

"Nothing?" he said.

I shook my head.

"Nothing is a suggestion, too, I suppose," he said. "Just as inaction is a form of action. Let me see the folder," and he reached for it, but I pulled it away.

"No," I said. I had second thoughts. Maybe I'd acted brashly, bringing over the poems without having worked on them at all.

"No?" He arched his eyebrows and regarded me suspiciously. "Let me see the folder."

I handed it to him. What else could I do? They were his

poems. He regarded the top poem silently for a minute, his hand cupped over his chin.

"Dr. Fischer," I said. I knew what I wanted to say, but I couldn't say it. Looking at him, I just felt pity. "I'm terrible," I said finally. "Can't you see that? I don't understand why you want me. Yesterday, I went to the library and spent half the day poring over Waley's translations and Anderson's. They seem fine to me."

His face darkened and he looked at me with astonishment. He flipped from one page to another.

"'A misty rain comes blowing with a wind from the east,'" Fischer announced suddenly. "Isn't it obvious what this refers to? Here, you've missed it," and he pointed to one of the translations.

Fischer leaned uncomfortably close and read over my shoulder. Even if I had been able to understand what he was talking about, I still couldn't have concentrated.

I didn't see it, whatever he was talking about, but nodded.

Fischer pointed to a poem called "Taking Leave of Wang Wei." I recognized the name Wang Wei. He was one of the Tang poets, too.

"This was written by Wang Wei's lover," Fischer told me.

"'I will turn back home, I will say no more,'" Fischer recited. "'I will close the gate of my old garden.'"

Dr. Fischer explained the image to me. This time, I couldn't hide my shock and I laughed. "You can't say that," I said.

"Of course not," Fischer said, and smiled. "What do you suggest?"

"It sounds fine the way it is. Garden. Why can't it just be a garden?" I bent over the manuscript and pointed at the word as though I had to prove it actually existed.

"I just don't see it," I said.

"You can't ignore it," Dr. Fischer said.

"Why does it have to be that way?" I asked. It was a garden. It said it was a garden. It didn't say anything about body parts.

The poem seemed fine to me without making something sexual out of it. It seemed like a simple poem about two friends saying good-bye, nothing more. And if it wasn't, I didn't have to know.

He started clearing the food-encrusted dishes from the table as though he'd just noticed them, as though I weren't there. He stacked them up and the cloud of flies broke up and then converged around his arms.

"Dr. Fischer," I said.

He didn't turn around to look at me, but kept stacking plates. "This is my work," he said. "These are my translations."

I didn't know exactly what to say. It occurred to me that it mattered. Until now, the poems hadn't seemed important. I thought that it was me. Actually, I hadn't gone to the library. I hadn't looked at anyone else's translations. I'd told him that so he'd think I was hardworking, but he seemed appalled.

Fischer disappeared into the kitchen and I heard him turn on the kitchen tap. I felt very thirsty.

Fischer walked into the dining room again. He pulled out a checkbook and a silver pen from his smelly jacket. "I want to pay you for today."

"For what?" I said. I shook my head. Dr. Fischer looked at me blankly. I pointed toward the kitchen. "May I have a glass of water?"

"There's bottled water in the refrigerator," he said.

The kitchen was covered with paintings and framed examples of calligraphy. I recognized another style from Dr. Fischer's slide lectures. If it was an original, it was hundreds and hundreds of years old. And priceless.

"Is this an original?" I asked.

"Do you like it?" he said, seeming to know which painting I referred to.

"It must be worth a fortune," I said.

I opened the refrigerator door. The light didn't turn on. The smell almost knocked me over. Most of the food was unidentifiable. There were several things wrapped in foil and a large bowl covered with green fuzz.

I shut the door, but the smell didn't subside. It engulfed me as I walked through the kitchen in search of a glass. I opened a cupboard and saw a box of saltines and three boxes of Mystic Mint cookies. That was all. There was no other food around. Plenty of glasses and plates, but nothing to fill them with. I checked every cupboard, every drawer.

I put my glass under the tap and let it run, testing the temperature with my finger. I filled the glass with cold water and drank so fast I had to stand there for a second and catch my breath. Then I filled it again and took my time.

I went into the dining room.

"Dr. Fischer," I said. "Why did you choose me?"

He paused and said, "Choose you for what?"

"For this. Translating these poems."

"Because you have a good ear, because you are honest, and because you are . . . American."

"How could you know I'm honest?" I said.

"At the restaurant. You speak bluntly. I admire that."

"But how could you tell I have a good ear? I just ran the slide projector for you."

"That doesn't matter," Fischer said. "It is your sensibility I wanted."

"You don't know my sensibility," I said.

"You were in my course. You were the boy who ran the slide projector. If my memory is correct, you earned an A?"

"You gave just about everyone an A, Dr. Fischer."

"Here," he said, handing me the check he'd made out. "Please don't cash it until Tuesday." I didn't take the check. With a kitchen like that, I was amazed that his previous check had cleared. He didn't have enough money for clothes. He couldn't afford food.

Fischer's cat Sophie jumped in his lap and he began to stroke her.

"I'm afraid you will be insulted," he said slowly, as though addressing his cat. "You see, you were the clumsiest calligrapher I've ever taught. You held the brush as though it were a meat hook. People see what they want to see. I am not so concerned about making these poems beautiful, but I want the true voices of the poets to be heard, even if I must peel them of all metaphor. In other words, my intent is to strip these poems of the subterfuge. If they are not obvious to you, then who will they be obvious to?"

What was he saying? That I was an oaf? I had appreciated the class, respected the work. So what if I didn't understand how to hold a brush, if all I was good for was advancing slides in a carousel?

"You said I was perfect."

"You were perfect," he said simply. "You couldn't handle the brush, but I thought you were sensitive. You gave a strong oral presentation. Do you remember?"

It was a video actually. I remembered. I did it back when I was sure what I was going to do with my life. The video was based on a famous Chinese poem. It showed a chair, a simple chair with a broken leg. The chair was in an empty white room and had toppled over. The camera panned around it as a woman's voice recited the English translation of the poem. As the poem was recited, the chair was slowly repaired, invisibly. First the leg was fixed and then a rich purple paint started to climb the legs to the back of the seat.

The poem was about an emperor whose enemies killed his favorite bride while he was away from the palace. His constant brooding for her turned the state into ruin, and so the people went to a Taoist priest, who was able to "summon spirits by his concentrated mind." The priest, searching for the woman among the pavilions and towers of the air, finally found her. He brought her back to earth in the form of a golden throne. Sitting on his throne, the emperor was strong and content, but when he was away from it, he could do nothing. And so he sat on the throne until his death, possessed by the spirit of his bride.

"I remembered this," Dr. Fischer said. "That's what I remembered when I asked for your help. Now I see you're a poseur, a dilettante. This is far worse than someone without ideas. You have good ideas, but you're afraid of them. I doubt you'll ever do anything with your life. I thought you would. I was sure of it."

He was right. Now I would have laughed at that emperor. I would have joked lewdly about him sitting on his wife. Or I would have told him he was sitting on a chair, nothing more, nothing less. How had this happened to me?

Fischer handed me the check, but I put my hand up.

"Take it," he said.

SERENADE

AFTER THE HUDSON VALLEY LINE BUS deposited Peter Draper at the crossroads that made up Cuddebackville, he had no choice but to walk the five miles to Mulligan Road and Sam's house. He couldn't remember ever having walked five miles before, and never with three suitcases. Nevertheless, he picked them up and crossed the small bridge beside the Cuddebackville Canal Store.

Peter had a habit of not planning well. He and his fiancée, Gretchen, had thought of this outing as more than a vacation: a retreat into the wilderness. They'd decided recently to get married but still had some doubts they needed to resolve, and what better way, they thought, than to isolate themselves, to devote their full attention to each other, and to hammer out those few remaining issues.

He was glad she wasn't with him now. He'd gone on ahead and Gretchen would join him in two days. She couldn't get the same dates off work as Peter, though that was all right, since this arrangement would give him a chance to check the place out and make sure it was livable. "The house is yours for two glorious weeks, you crazy lovebirds," his cousin Sam Waldorf had written from L.A. "Make it alive again and make love in every room of the house for good luck. The house will appreciate the gesture."

Sam's house stood in the middle of nowhere in the foothills of the Catskills. Over a hundred years old, it had served originally as a farmhouse, then as a boardinghouse for not-so-wealthy vacationers who couldn't afford to stay at the Concord, up the road about thirty miles. Sam proudly called the house the Waldorf Hysteria. The house hadn't been lived in for five years, the victim of Sam and his ex-wife Julia's divorce. They'd both decided to hang onto the house together as a vacation spot, but Sam, who lived now in L.A., never visited it, and Julia, whose career in New York as a fashion photographer was thriving, could never find the time. So they sent out an all-points bulletin to the rest of the clan, far-flung between the two coasts of Sam and Julia's failed marriage. Anyone who had the will and a way to find Cuddebackville could make use of the premises, on the condition they leave the house in better shape than they found it.

As Peter struggled across the bridge, he had the feeling this was happening to him for the second time, though he'd never before set foot in Cuddebackville. The bridge spanned the Delaware and Hudson Canal, or what remained of it. A century ago, the canal had bustled with commerce. There wasn't any use for it anymore and most of it had choked up and turned to pasture. Here, the canal was nothing more than a black pool. Across the road, the canal widened into a pond, and next to it sat an abandoned mill with its windows and doors rotted out.

This was no ordinary déjà vu. It had some basis in fact. Two years earlier, he'd planned this same trip with his old girlfriend Susan, not Gretchen. The purpose of the trip had been slightly different, not a two-week retreat before marriage (they hadn't been engaged), but simply a getaway. Susan wasn't a planner either, and had lived purely by intuition. Gretchen didn't know much about Susan, only the bleak facts of what had happened to her.

It all happened over one summer, three bad turns, any one of which Susan might have shaken off. But Susan had always seemed one step from the edge anyway. First, Susan had lost her job, a sudden layoff, and despondent, wouldn't look for another. Then her parents decided to split up. Barely a month after that, her friend Caroline committed suicide. Two days after Caroline died, Susan received a letter from her. It reminded Susan of the twenty-five dollars she had borrowed, and instructed her to pay the money to Caroline's mother. The letter, combined with everything else, completely shattered Susan. She started to think *she* had killed Caroline. Peter tried to convince Susan that the letter meant nothing, that it was the product of a sick and despairing girl. It wasn't, as Susan believed, a pointing finger from the spirit world, a subtle accusation.

Gretchen didn't know much more about Susan than that. She definitely didn't know that he'd once planned on going to Cuddebackville with Susan. If he *had* mentioned anything to Gretchen, she wouldn't have agreed to make the trip. He had no doubts about this. She wanted everything they did to be new, theirs alone.

A small truck pulled up beside him and a large man in a blue blazer leaned toward him and said, "Need a lift?"

Peter threw his suitcases in the back and hopped in. The man smiled and they shook hands. He was a high-school teacher in Port Jervis, heading home, only two miles away, but he knew where Mulligan Road was and offered to drive Peter right to the doorstep. The road they traveled was only two lanes and wound alongside the

Neversink River, which looked shallow and strewn with hundreds of boulders and smaller rocks, over which the water coursed. On the way, they also passed a tiny cemetery and a smattering of trailers and ranch-style houses with wooden rail fences, barking dogs, and satellite dishes. The high-school teacher pointed out a small red building that he said had once been a one-room schoolhouse. Now it stood abandoned, like so much else around here.

They traded stories, filling in the bare facts of their lives. Peter told the man he was twenty-five, that he worked as a tech writer in the city but had majored in film at Columbia. And Peter told him why he was in Cuddebackville. He mentioned Gretchen, that she did word processing at a law firm where they were slave drivers, and wouldn't allow her to take off two days early. Of course, he also mentioned that they were getting married.

The man smiled and congratulated him, and said he hoped they had a long and happy life together. For his part, he confided, things had not gone so well. He and his wife had recently separated after twenty years of marriage, but he said he was starting to adjust. Things were looking up. He was putting the past behind him. Peter nodded in sympathy, even more so because the man was so transparent. He didn't have the look of someone who was adjusting. He looked frightened and uncertain.

Still, Peter was glad for the company. He'd never been this alone, or at least as alone as he imagined he'd be until Gretchen arrived. By nature, he enjoyed other people's company. Sometimes, he didn't even care whose company he was in, just so he didn't have to be alone. For the last week, he'd been so keyed up about being cut off from Gretchen and everyone else that his sleep had been spotty; he'd suffered through a steady succession of nightmares, vivid ones that lingered after he awakened, souring part of the day.

After a while, they turned onto Mulligan Road, which crossed the Neversink and went up a steep hill. The light changed on this road, which was thrown into shadow by the large trees on either side. Peter noticed cocoons in almost all the trees.

"Gypsy moths," the man told him, shaking his head. "Big problem this year. They're completely stripping all the trees. I hope you have a hat because they'll be dropping on you like rain."

No, he hadn't brought a hat. This was something else he hadn't foreseen, but maybe dumb luck would help him the way it had helped him get a ride, and he'd find some kind of cap in the house.

There wasn't much else on Mulligan Road but trees and cocoons. They passed only one house, a large one with a huge lawn. Frank Mulligan, the man for whom the road was named, owned this house. Frank owned half the county, according to Sam. He and his wife, Babe, were in their mid-seventies, and Frank had been born in the house that Sam now owned. Frank had supposedly turned on the electricity for Peter, and had hooked up the phone, too.

Half a mile farther, they found the Waldorf Hysteria. A gray metal mailbox on a pole read *Waldorf*, and beyond that was a deep lawn with knee-high grass. Cutting the lawn, he knew, would be one of his primary duties here, and that wouldn't be a simple task. First, he'd have to master Sam's Gravely tractor, stored out in the large red barn beside the road. There wasn't any guarantee it would work, no guarantee that anything would work.

Peter thanked the man, took his suitcases out of the back, and staggered across the lawn toward the house, which was even larger than he'd expected.

The screen door was wide open and the main door was open a crack. He walked in and put his suitcases down, appalled by what he saw.

The ceiling of the living room had caved in, exposing pipes. The whole room had a fetid, slightly sweet smell, and the first thing Peter did was force open a window. Stepping over plaster, he walked a little farther into the room, which looked like it had been frozen in the 1960s. Posters of movies and plays from that time decorated the walls: *Midnight Cowboy; Zoo Story; Oh Dad, Poor Dad, Mama's Hung You in the Closet and I'm Feelin' So Sad; King of Hearts*. A console TV stood in the corner with an antenna and an aluminum-foil flag attached. There were also a sofa and a daybed in the room, both covered with filthy Day-Glo covers. Apparently, some kind of animal had been living in here; the beds had piles of desiccated animal droppings on top.

Something came toward him from the kitchen. A large tomcat, probably the largest in the world, rushed him with wild eyes. It howled at Peter, who howled back and jumped aside. The animal sped past him and out the open door. He clutched his hand to his chest and tried to breathe normally. Apparently, he had just confronted the current owner of the house. Peter went to the door and shut it.

He noticed something in the corner by the TV. He walked closer and saw a dead bird propped up against the wall, facing the TV as though its blank black eyes were watching. The bird had a vivid yellow belly and all its feathers were intact, fluffed up but motionless. A little bird mummy, perfectly preserved. The cat had probably caught the bird, killed it, and somehow, in the midst of play, propped it against the wall.

How strange, he thought, and then his second thought was that he had a lot of work ahead if he wanted to get the house in order before Gretchen arrived. She'd kill him if the place was still a wreck by the time she showed up. Susan, of course, would have been a different story. She would have been intrigued by the dead bird, the cat, all of it. She would have seen meaning in all this. He wondered how long the house had looked this way, how long the bird had been propped against the wall, the ceiling had been caved in, the cat had been living here. He wondered, if he and Susan had made it this far, would they have encountered what he was encountering now? After all, the house had been unoccupied for five years, and he and Susan had planned the same trip only two years earlier.

He had promised himself he wasn't going to think about Susan, that she wasn't going to interfere with his vacation. Yet he couldn't help hear her tell him the bird was some kind of mystic sign, and the cat a witch's familiar. That's the way Susan thought, at least after Caroline's suicide, when she tumbled into paranoia and started seeing everything as a sign.

Once, on the subway, she'd tugged on his arm and told him they had to get out at a stop that wasn't theirs. He'd done it. He assumed there was a good reason because she was so afraid. On the platform, when he asked her why, she told him that Caroline's mother had hired some men to kill her and she'd seen them on the train.

He stopped and stared at her. He took her by the shoulders and begged her to see someone, but she refused, became infuriated, told him he wasn't really her friend.

Susan's decline took place slowly over an entire summer, but in Peter's memory it seemed like a day and no more. He remembered awakening alone one night and Susan was gone, the front door wide open. He stayed up, pacing, wondering what to do. At dawn, he called her father and told him what was happening to Susan, that she needed help but wouldn't get any. He could tell by his tone of voice that Susan's father didn't believe him. It was patient and controlled, the way you'd handle someone less fortunate than yourself. "I'll come visit in a couple of months," the man said. "Just have her call me when she gets back. If you knew what I'd been through with Susan, this wouldn't seem like anything."

Susan didn't return until noon. She announced that she'd been touched by the Spirit, that she knew how to lead her life now.

None of these thoughts, of course, was doing him any good, so he stepped past the little bird mummy into the kitchen, an airy room almost as big as his apartment, with plenty of cabinets and windows. The kitchen abutted a dining room with windows that looked off into an immense pasture, and beyond that, miles of distant blue hills. The kitchen also led onto a screened porch that stretched the length of the house. There were sun chairs with foamy cushions on the porch, and two piles of bocci balls, one green, one red. From the porch, he went back into the house and crossed the dining room, which led into another smaller porch on the other side of the house. Here, too, was a room with piles of junk in it, tools and boxes of books, and a Ping-Pong table in the center. Beyond this room was a den with a fireplace, but it was not an inviting room. It had heavy blinds on the windows, and the feeling in the room was dark and close. In the corner stood an upright Victrola with a seventy-eight on the turntable. He read the label, a song he'd never heard of called "Cigareets and Whiskey and Wild, Wild Women." Beside the Victrola stood a megaphone. He picked it up and brought it to his lips, but didn't say anything. On one side of the room was a door leading to a dilapidated carport. A door on the other side of the room led back to the main entrance and the stairs. He climbed the stairs and discovered four bedrooms, a bathroom, and two more thrush mummies. One was in a window sill, the other on one of the beds.

After lugging his suitcases to the cleanest of the bedrooms, he returned to the kitchen to search for food. The cupboards were completely bare except for one box of Girl Scout cookies. Obviously, the cookies were at least five years old, but he was hungry, so he opened the box and bit into one.

It had a faint sugary taste. It was absolutely dry and crumbled in his mouth. It seemed more like five thousand years old than five, as though this had been a Girl Scout cookie of the Pharaohs. He glanced at the box for a freshness date.

The cookie sucked all the moisture from him and left him feeling choked and unable to swallow. He went to the sink and blew crumbs into it, then turned on the tap. Something brown and sludgy chugged out of the tap and stuck to the bottom of the sink. Nothing more came out.

Yet another example of poor planning on his part, and he berated himself for it. He said it out loud, realizing that he was completely alone, and that he could say anything and in a sense it would be just the same as saying it in his mind, because no one else could hear him. He said, "You stupid jerk. You should have picked up some food at the Cuddebackville Canal Store."

He said it again. And once more. His words, any words, filled up the emptiness of the house. Then he realized what he was doing, and he stopped, and the silence in the house seemed more silent than before.

Susan had talked to herself—not at first, of course, not when he first knew her, but later. She'd walk around her apartment mumbling to herself, half of the time completely unaware of Peter's presence. When she noticed him, she rushed up, clutching her tiny Bible with its green plastic cover, the Bible she'd picked up at the sidewalk mission. Then she'd open it up, seemingly at random, and say, "See here, Peter. This is us! This is you and me: 'All the commandments which I command you this day you shall be careful to do, that you may live and multiply, and go in and possess the land which the Lord swore to give to your fathers. And you shall remember all the way which the Lord your God has led you these forty years in the wilderness, that he might humble you, testing you to know what was in your heart, whether you would keep his commandments, or not.'"

Of course, nothing she read ever had anything to do with them, and he tried to tell her so, but she'd just close the Bible and touch it lightly to her lips, then continue with her mumblings and rantings, her frantic attempts at atonement for something that wasn't her fault in the first place.

Before he could start cleaning up, he needed to walk all the way back to Cuddebackville to get some groceries. The first four miles weren't bad. For a while, he walked the banks of the Neversink, stopped by the tiny cemetery and read the names and dates. One set of graves fascinated him. They were the graves of three infants from the same family, all named Joseph Jr., the dates of their deaths only a year apart. Three times the parents had tried to give their child his father's name, and three times the children hadn't survived. The parents' graves weren't there, and Peter stood for a long time wondering what might have happened to them—perhaps they'd moved away, perhaps they'd succeeded on a fourth try, perhaps they'd both gone mad with grief, or perhaps the mother had run off with another man and had a clan of children, none named Joseph Jr.

By the time he'd walked four miles, he thought he'd actually walked five, even six or seven, and he expected to see the little Cuddebackville Canal Store at any moment. He'd forgotten to look for a cap, and he had to keep brushing gypsy caterpillars out of his hair.

An occasional car passed by, and he stuck out his thumb, but no one picked him up. Even though there was plenty of room between him and their cars, the drivers would swerve wildly around him into the other lane, as though they didn't even want him within twenty feet.

Finally, he reached the store, exhausted, his daydreams played out.

"Hello," he said when he entered the small room with a plank floor and three sparse rows of groceries. Up front near the cash register stood a white metal rack of postcards. Two men, both about sixty and dressed in jeans and T-shirts, wandered among the warped shelves, not paying him any attention. No one else occupied the room, but Peter saw an open door into a small room behind the cash register. The light and sound of a TV filtered out.

"Is anyone around?" Peter asked the two men, meaning, Is anyone working here? But the men seemed to think he was asking an existential question. They went about their business, ignoring him completely. Peter, who was good-natured, didn't easily accept the ill will of others, and generally gave people as many chances to hurt him as they could stand.

"What do you want?" a voice behind him said.

He turned and saw a bony woman with her hair pulled tight in back. The woman had large ears, big lips, and a jutting chin, but tiny eyes, a small nose, and the smallest forehead Peter had ever seen. Her hair seemed to begin where her eyebrows ended.

"I'm going to be spending a couple of weeks up at Sam Waldorf's place on Mulligan Road," he told her as she looked him up and down. "I'll probably come in here often for food," he added, figuring that might awaken her entrepreneurial spirit enough to smile at him. She looked at him as if he were insane, as if he'd just walked into her store naked and started babbling. She watched him as if he might be capable of anything, and had to be watched constantly.

She ran her tongue between her upper lip and her front teeth, and her face became chimplike.

Peter turned around. The two farmers had vanished and there wasn't any movement in the store except for the dust in the air, illuminated by a single band of sun on the floor.

Under the woman's intense scrutiny, he shopped. He bought what he thought he could carry: a quart of skim milk, a plastic liter of diet soda, a loaf of spongy white bread (the only kind in the store), several cans of soup, five cans of tuna, one of sardines, a bag of pretzels, some American-cheese slices, and a box of frozen chicken patties. He realized, however, that he hadn't checked to see if the stove or the refrigerator was working. After all, Sam *had* told him that the water was supposedly turned on. Tomorrow, he'd have to go over to Frank Mulligan's house, introduce himself, and ask him for a little help turning on the water. For now, unsure whether he could even cook his frozen chicken patties, he decided to buy a few other things that didn't need cooking. The vegetables were poor-quality, but he picked up a head of wilted lettuce and some scraggly carrots. He also purchased a can opener, another thing he hadn't checked at the house.

The woman packed everything in a large brown paper bag, but she placed the bread on the bottom and stacked the soup on top of it. "Careful," he couldn't stop himself from saying. She stopped and glared at him, then continued with her haphazard packing.

After Peter had walked over two miles cradling his cumbersome sack of groceries, his arms felt like they were going to wither and drop off. But he continued on.

He walked across the field in front of the one-room school-house and peered inside. There wasn't much: a room with a fire-place and a wooden floor. The room was in pretty good condition except for a stain, perhaps a burn mark, in front of the fireplace. He remembered finding Susan kneeling in the center of her floor one day, staring at a similar stain in the wood and mumbling.

"What are you doing?" he had said.

She told him the stain was the sign of the devil. He told her that it had been there since she'd moved in, but she wouldn't budge.

Not only was this the devil's sign, but now she claimed that the devil was going to kill her. She even knew when: at two that morning. Her certainty had chilled him, and he said, "No he's not. I won't let him."

"There's nothing you can do," she said, and turned away from him, still mumbling her prayers at the floor.

Peter went to the kitchen and took all the knives from the drawers. He carried them to the closet and threw them in back and buried them with clothes. Then he went to the phone and called Susan's father in front of Susan, and put her on the phone so her father could know the state she was in. That finally convinced him, and he agreed to fly out the next day and bring Susan home.

Still, they had to get through the night. He was so afraid for her that neither of them slept. The deadline passed and nothing happened. So she set another deadline. The devil was going to kill her at three that morning. When three o'clock arrived, she changed it to four. And on it went until five in the afternoon of the next day, when Susan's father arrived.

Clouds, which seemed to appear from nowhere, opened up, and rain and hail fell on Peter with twice the force and a hundred times the frequency of the gypsy moth caterpillars that had dropped on his head. He picked up his sack and hurried on. After a mile, the bag started disintegrating in his arms. Rain ran down either side of his face and off his chin. As the bag fell apart, Peter cradled the cans and bread and milk in his stretched-out shirt, looking down at them as he walked. It was heavy and awkward, and he had to keep his hands in place or everything would fall. Occasionally, he heard a car approach and turned around, but since he couldn't take his hands away, he couldn't thumb a ride. All he could do was jerk his head as the car approached, but this did no good. The cars swerved even farther away, and he couldn't blame them. Here was a hunched man walking in the rain, exposing his stomach and twitching his head. They probably thought he'd risen from the black pool of the D & H Canal.

He had almost reached Mulligan Road when his foot kicked the chin of a deer and it looked up at him. Of course, it was looking

up anyway, but he didn't know that, and he screamed and his groceries landed in a circle around the dead deer.

He didn't know what to do, so he started gathering his food
again. The bread had landed in the V of the deer's stiff front legs,
on a tuft of white fur. He left it there. If he touched the deer, it
would touch him in some way, become part of him, and he didn't
want that. Besides, there were diseases, and he had no water at home
with which to clean himself.

He was able to salvage only half of what he had bought. The
rest belonged to the dead deer now, and the deer belonged to the
wet ground.

Standing in the rain, his groceries at his feet in a pile like the
bocci balls on the porch of the house, he chopped the air with his
hand, water pouring down his face, and yelled, "Okay, what is going on? Why are you doing this to me?"

He closed his eyes and saw Susan's face so clear and immediate
that it startled him almost as much as coming across the deer. He
wanted to tell her something, to say, "It wasn't my fault," but she
wasn't really there and so he didn't say anything. There wasn't any
point in it. Even if he'd wanted to talk to Susan now, he wouldn't
have known how. After Susan's father flew her home to Dallas and
placed her in a hospital, Susan called him from the hospital every
day, but all she did was preach. He couldn't get her to talk about
anything else, except that she hated her psychiatrist, that they'd put
her in a straitjacket on the first day when she tried to run from
them, and that nothing was wrong with her. She blamed her father,
but strangely she didn't blame Peter at all. She spoke sweetly, con-
spiratorially, as though Peter alone among her family and friends
knew the truth that she was sane.

They stayed in touch, but all she talked was religion. She wanted
to convert him. One day, Susan wrote him a letter that said she'd
been drinking a glass of water and had finished half when it sud-

denly filled again. "Christ does things like that to me sometimes," she wrote. "He's so mysterious. I like having him around."

Finally, Peter told her she had to talk about something else, and she said sadly, "I wish you could enter my world." After that, she didn't call him again, and he didn't call or write. He knew what he was doing. She was in bad shape. He was abandoning her, consciously, and forever.

Back at the house, he removed all his sopping clothes, and because he was completely alone, didn't bother to unpack any dry ones from his suitcase. He placed his clothes in a pile between the mummified thrush and the blank TV, stripping down completely. Then he walked though the house and turned on every light in every room. He was embarrassed not because of his nudity but because something frightened him, and he wasn't sure what.

He found the broom closet, removed what he needed, and swept the dead thrush into a dustpan, then tossed it out into the yard. Outside, the night was darker than any he was used to. He could see no lights from any other buildings. He could not see the road in front of his house.

He found the other thrushes and tossed them in the same direction as the first. And that was the extent of his cleaning. He didn't want to spend the night with thrush mummies, but he was too exhausted to even think about cleaning anything else.

He went to the side porch and, still naked, started to read a book he'd brought with him, one he'd always wanted to read but had never found time for. He wanted to engross himself in the book, to shed his uneasiness, but after a few pages he felt restless and wandered inside again.

He surveyed the living room, the collapsed ceiling, the posters frozen in another decade. He happened to look up at the stairs and shuddered. No matter what, he thought, I can't let myself think the house is haunted.

Of course, as soon as he thought that, he couldn't get the notion out of his mind. He even knew who was haunting the house. Someone who'd lived here many years before. He couldn't see the landing from where he stood, but he imagined her standing at the top, waiting to descend.

He knew this was mad. He needed to get some sleep. Maybe he'd call Gretchen to let her know he'd arrived safely. More or less. The phone, he discovered when he lifted it from its cradle, had not been connected. Still, he kept it by his ear and listened to nothing.

He replaced the phone and stood up. "I'm alone," he said aloud. "It doesn't matter what anyone else thinks. It doesn't matter if I'm imagining things. No one will ever know."

He walked to the stairs, stood nude at the foot of them, and announced, "Look, we both have to live here together for a couple of weeks. I don't mean to disturb you. I promised my cousin Sam I'd leave the house in better condition than I found it."

He didn't wait for an answer. He didn't want an answer. What he wanted was some kind of diversion.

He walked to the den and cranked the Victrola. He placed the heavy tonearm on the record, but it skidded across with a violent scratching. He set the tonearm back and listened. He stared at the unlit fireplace, the empty chairs. The darkness seemed to be closing in, and he knew that the ghost behind him was slowly descending, making her way toward him. He didn't even need to turn around. He felt the silence, the weight of her presence. He listened but couldn't hear it, knew that she didn't need to be heard to be known.

Then he noticed the megaphone standing beside the Victrola. He picked it up and brought it to his lips. He thought he should sing, that this was the only solution, that the ghost just wanted to hear something sweet, something to remind her of being alive, of all that had meant. But what song? Nothing came to mind, and he felt that he was almost out of time, that she had almost reached the bottom of the stairs, that soon she would tap him lightly on the shoulder and take him. She would ask him a question that he wouldn't be able to bear.

As she drew her hand out in front, he remembered something, a song, a simple one from the twenties he used to croon to Susan before her trouble began. Back then, he'd look at her when he sang, and it made him feel they'd always be together. He sang it now, marching through the electrically blazing house, crooning in the wilderness, fearless and certain he was doing some good, appeasing someone. The ghost danced and spun to his tune but didn't show herself, and didn't frighten Peter anymore.

Back in the living room, he stopped and listened. He closed his eyes and smiled ecstatically. He didn't need to see himself. He knew how wild he must look, how crazy his behavior must seem to the outside world in the dark. What did he care? He felt like it *was* a hundred years from now, and none of what he had done before mattered. In a hundred years, his whole life would be like tonight. No one could know the mystery of it. No one would see.

He tried to imagine, eyes closed, what it would be like a hundred years from now, what new people would live in this house, if it still stood. Maybe by then people would leave it in better shape than they'd found it, which after all was Sam's one simple request. He imagined himself standing before those people, though they couldn't see him. And they'd wonder, too, what life had been like a hundred years ago. What would they imagine from his time? A little music on the wind. Some insignificant gesture.

He climbed the stairs to bed, naked, with megaphone in hand, and dreamed all night long. He didn't remember a single one in the morning.